Unfulfilled

L. Charmane Pough Chestnut

1st WORLD
PUBLISHING

Unfulfilled

L. Charmane Pough Chestnut

© L. Charmane Pough Chestnut 2008

Published by 1stWorld Publishing
P.O. Box 2211 Fairfield, Iowa 52556
tel: 641-209-5000 • fax: 641-209-3001
web: www.1stworldpublishing.com

First Edition

LCCN: 2008943713
SoftCover ISBN: 978-1-4218-9055-5
HardCover ISBN: 978-1-4218-9054-8
eBook ISBN: 978-1-4218-9056-2

PROVERBS 13: 12
HOPE DEFERRED MAKETH THE HEART SICK,
BUT WHEN THE DESIRE COMETH IT IS A TREE
OF LIFE

"HOPE"—TO LOOK FORWARD TO
OR TO HAVE A FEELING THAT WHAT IS WANTED
OR DESIRE WITH REASONABLE CONFIDENCE
CAN BE HAD!!!

"FAITH"—CONFIDENCE OR TRUST IN A PERSON
OR THING, BELIEF IN GOD!!!

"REALITY"—THE STATE OR QUALITY OF BEING
REAL, FACTS OR EVENTS AS A WHOLE!!!

In Memory of

I would like to dedicate this book in loving memory of my parents Harold and Lillian Colter Pough, who gave me life and nurtured me, until their demise. You instilled in me Godly morals and the love of Jesus Christ.

My grandparents, Rev. Clifton and Daisey Walker Colter and Mozell and Anna Jamison Pough who were the root of all my endeavors.

In addition, my precious niece, little Miss Porchia DaShaune Holmes, my angel, you brought so much joy to my life the few years you were here. I miss and love all of you so much.

Acknowledgments

...I offer sincere gratitude and praise to my Lord and Savior Jesus Christ, who is the author and the finisher of my faith, He has started a good work in me and He is faithful to complete it. You have always believed in me. You turned my mourning into dancing and gave me beauty for ashes. Though weeping may endure for night, I thank you that joy comes in the morning...I love you with all of my heart.

...My husband Sandaeaud (Sandy) Sr., and my sons Sandaeaud Jr., Marquise T. Sandtel R. Chestnut, who have been an enormous support and inspiration, Thank you so much.

...Too my mother-n-law Minerva Gray, my brothers and sisters, Jerry, Alvin (Diane), Freddie, and Kelly Colter, Harold (Diane) Pough, Harold Lee, Kenny and Gail Jenkins, Sammy, Robert (LaQuitta) Gray, and Sabrina (Henry) Rugg, Percy O Greaves, thank you for believing in me.

...I give thanks to an innumerable amount of people, who has catapulted me into this next dimension in my life.

...Thanks to my Pastors Elder Cardell and Lady Carolyn Sutton and the entire New Life Outreach Ministries, of Swansea, South Carolina, where Men are Strengthened, Women are Restored and Families are Made Whole. You have really stirred up the gift in me. Thanks to Pastors Alonzo and Lady Angel Gerald and the entire Allow God Ministries of Suitland, Maryland, for being steadfast in "The devil cannot stop God from Blessing Me."

...Too Sabrina Johnson Coates for being my forerunner and Author of "Anointed Flow" Too my friends Roslyn (John) Bush, Henrietta (Adrian) Robinson, Maurice & Faith Griffin, we talked, argued, cried, and laugh. When I wanted to give up, you would not let me. I truly thank you for how you stood firm and for the timeless hours, you invested in me.

...My special nieces Lillian (MJ) & Glenshay Colter & Porchia Jones, nephew Brian Colter, my cousin Marilyn Inabinette and Chandra Yon-Corley who is always concerned about me. In addition, Racquel King, thank you for being you in such a unique way. Also, my auntie who would tell you that I am her favorite niece, Earnellar (Sister) Jackson, I love you. ...Thanks to Janie Byrd and Sean Reese and the crew in Beltsville Maryland, you have always given me a good laugh. Thank you Emma Perry, Gwendolyn Jackson, Josephine Thomas, Charmaine Shim Chow Min, Detrius Williams, Cathy Jones, Lillian Washington, Sandy Wilder, Regina Davis, Marilyn Davis, and Joyce Harrison we have had so much fun together.

...Too my marketing team, Nicholas & Yvette Gillcrese, Veronica Gordon and Tarsha Jeffcoat, thank you for all of your hard work and To Cynthia Pace Photography, thanks for the beautiful photos, and Davis and Dingle for the beautiful smile.

...In addition, Leah Walker, Sarah Neate and Ed Spinella and the entire 1st World Publishing Co. Thank you for supporting and giving me the opportunity to share my vision.

... Too all of my aunts, uncles, cousins, nieces and nephews, friends and associates and last but not least my enemies (haters). I thank you for you love and support. I love all of you so much. Too God be the glory for what He is doing! "For His Divine Purpose is being manifested in my life."

Chapter One

July 5

SHAYMIN awoke to the ringing phone.

"Morning," she said, feeling groggy and hung over.

Joshua and Roché Jenkins always had their annual July 4 party, and Shaymin never missed it. But every time she attended their party, or any other party, she would wake up the next morning in the same state—hung over and sick as a dog.

"Heeeey Roché." Shaymin paused then said, "You know the same ole, same ole, my head hurts, my stomach hurts and I do not know who the hell is lying in my bed beside me. Roché, who brought me home last night? Whoever it was, he is still lying in my bed this morning. Girl, why would you allow me to drive home last night? You know I always over-do it at anybody's party, and as always, I am paying for it this morning. Girl, I will call you back after I find out who this two-time joker laying in my bed beside me is."

"Okay Shaymin," Roché said. "Holler at me later."

"Hey!" Shaymin yelled to the man beside her. "Who the hell are you? Actually, what are you doing in my bed? Ouch!" She squeezed her eyes as her head began to pound.

"Good morning, baby!" the man smiled. "How do you feel this morning, and did you sleep well last night?" He nodded. "You lured me into your car last night. You said you wanted a real man to wake up beside you."

Shaymin shamefully turned around to look at him. "So what did you do to me last night?" she asked.

With a big grin, he answered, "Everything you wanted and asked for... So how do you feel baby? Was it good to you?"

Oh no, you two timing hypocrite! Shaymin thought. What will I tell Carlos? He is away on a business trip until Tuesday. I know I am promiscuous and flirtatious, but how could I have slept with someone I don't even know? I have never seen this joker, at least not that I remember. He is lying comfortably in my bed right now. Mmm, she thought as she glanced at him, he looks to be fine as all outdoors: approximately 6'3", nice and chocolaty, and well groomed. Plus he has a gap in his front teeth, which will grab my attention on even the ugliest person in town.

"What's your name?" she asked.

"Roger Thanksgiving." He continued, "I am thankful to have given you everything you asked for last night and I will oblige if you want a repeat. How about a second round?" He massaged his mustache. "Umm, I am sorry baby what did you say your name is?"

"My name is Shaymin Cumbersome, and I cannot believe you actually raped me last night," she rattled off.

"No," Roger replied softly, "I would not stoop so low as to rape you. I am a real man remember. At least that is what you told me last night. Also, real men don't rape, they fulfill your every need and want, your every desire, and your every fantasy."

He gently massaged her hand and continued, "So Shaymin, after all that we did last night, are you telling me you do not remember anything? I can press rewind and we can play last night all over again."

Shaymin shrugged her shoulders. "No," she replied. "How could you have done this to me? I was drunk. I do not even remember seeing you at the party, yet alone inviting you to my house. Oh shoot," she paused, "how can I explain this to Carlos?"

"Who is Carlos?" Roger asked.

"Carlos is my fiancé; we are engaged to be married in ten months. May 8 of next year to be exact."

Roger sighed, "You are engaged to be married, and you are inviting strange men into your home. That is very dangerous, sweetie. How often do you take on dangerous acts like this? You could have been raped or killed last night and no one would have ever known what happened to you."

Roger smiled, "Listen baby, tell Carlos you playfully dared me to get into your car last night, and I could not let you down. You took me home with you and we had the time of your life. Then Carlos will be gone, and you can become my wife."

"Aww, be for real Carl—I mean Roger," Shaymin replied.

"See I already have you calling me your fiancé's name. You know you want some more of me don't you?" Roger teased her.

Shaymin shamefully massaged her temples quietly for a few minutes; her head was pounding even more now as she sat thinking, I really like this handsome hunk of a man who says I lured him into my car last night.

She said aloud, "C'mon Roger, tell me the truth, whose friend or associate are you? Why were you at the party alone? And why did you choose me to take advantage of?"

Roger laughed. "Shaymin! One question at a time, please. How about I take you to breakfast and we can talk about last night and our future together."

"Future?" Shaymin questioned him. "We do not have a future together. I told you I am engaged to be married May of next year, and you are not the one I am going to marry."

"Wanna bet?" Roger replied.

"I do not bet," Shaymin answered.

"Okay, so how about breakfast? But first, may I please use your restroom?"

"Sure, down the hallway to your left, second door on the right."

Shaymin noticed as he rose out of bed that he was fully dressed. He's bowlegged too, she thought as he strode to the restroom. My, my, my.

When Roger returned from the restroom, he smiled and she almost melted; she found herself really attracted to Mr. Tall, Dark, and Handsome.

"Breakfast?" he asked.

"Yes," Shaymin said. "I need to take a shower. I will be ready in about forty-five minutes."

Shaymin took a very hot shower, and tried to remember

some of the previous night. Unfortunately, she could not remember anything. She really was hung over and did not feel up to going to breakfast, but she decided she would go because she liked Roger, and she wanted to find out what had happened last night.

Shaymin came downstairs in her peach sleeveless capri-pant outfit and some peach flip-flops. She had pulled her hair back into a ponytail and added eyeliner, lip liner, mascara, and peach lipstick to complement her outfit.

"Wow," Roger said, "you look stunning." He continued, "Shaymin baby, can you take me to Joshua and Roché's house so I can get my car? Then I'll drive us to my house so I can change and we can go to breakfast."

Shaymin and Roger got into her 2002 XJS Series Jaguar. It was bronze with lightly tinted windows, a sunroof, and five-star rims.

"Nice car," Roger said.

"Carlos bought it for my birthday this year. It has always been my dream car, and Carlos aims to please me. He wants me to have any and everything my heart desires. Carlos is my sweet cup of tea; he loves to shop for me. Anytime he is away on a business trip, he brings me back some elaborate gift. It is always a great surprise."

Shaymin got very quiet. Sometimes I wonder why I am so unhappy, she thought. I have everything a woman could want or desire. I have a man who loves me, who has asked for my hand in marriage. Why, why am I so unhappy?

"Are you happy?" Roger asked.

"Yes, I am happy," she lied quickly.

Roger replied, "I find that hard to believe after talking to you last night. However, the truth will come out. Material things are a temporary fix, a short-term form of happiness. Real happiness comes from within."

Why would he think I am unhappy? She asked herself as she gazed out of the window. What did I do or say last night? I am truly ashamed of myself.

"Shaymin, are you okay?" Roger asked as he smiled at her.

"Yes," she replied, "just thinking about Carlos and his returning home on Tuesday. I wonder what he will have for me this time. Oh how I love him."

Chapter Two

"HEY ROCHÉ," Shaymin said as Roché invited them into her gorgeous, six-bedroom, state-of-the-art mansion. It had four baths, a living room, dining room, family room, children's game room, and entertainment room with theater seating and surround-sound 63" flat-screen television. There was a three-car garage to park their 2000 royal blue Suburban, 1998 silver BMW, and 2001 X JS Series black Jaguar.

"Where are my girls Blessing and Amen?" Shaymin asked.

"They are upstairs. Mom brought them home about an hour ago," Roché replied. "You know they would love to see their Auntie Shay."

"Yes, I will make sure I kiss them before I leave," Shaymin said.

"Shaymin," Roché said as she looked over her reading glasses and winked her eye, "can you tell me who, what, when, and why?"

"Hello," Roger's deep baritone voice came from behind Shaymin. "My name is Roger Thanksgiving. I am Jody Cockwell's partner, from Cockwell & Thanksgiving Law Firm. Joshua knows me from the office and invited me to the awesome party you hosted last night. I really appreciated everything. The food was great and your hospitality deserves a standing ovation." As he spoke, he gently took Roché's hand to his mouth and placed a soft kiss on it. "My Nubian princess, thank you.

"By the way," Roger smiled, "where is Joshua? I mean Mr. Jenkins. Is he home?"

"Yes, he is here. Josh baby," Roché yelled, "there is someone here to see you, a Mr. Thanksgiving."

"Please, call me Roger," he said.

As Roger strode across the hardwood kitchen floor, Shaymin looked at Roché and Roché looked at Shaymin. They said simultaneously, "Fine!"

Roché laughed, "You have some questions to answer, girl-friend."

"I plead the fifth," Shaymin responded with a big grin. "I do not remember anything. You know me, I get drunk and fall out and remember nothing after drink number five. But, but, but," she shook her head and blinked her eyes provoca-tively, "if what I see is as good as what I see, I must, I shall, I got to go out with him..."

"Sober!" they said in unison.

"Can you blame me?" Shaymin asked.

"No. He is all of that, a bag of chips, a drink, and a desert on the side." They both laughed.

Shaymin said as she shook her head, "So, soooo sorry that

you are married and cannot have anybody but Josh."

"And you my dear Shaymin, are betrothed to be married to Carlos on May 8 of next year," Roché replied.

"Yeah, yeah," Shaymin smiled. "I know." She raised her hands in the air as if praising the Lord. "But as Pastor Shelton always says, how many more praises do you have? One more! So can I have just one more Roger before I get married? Hallelujah!"

"Girl you are crazy," Roché replied.

"I may be crazy," said Shaymin, "but I am not blind. I like what I see and what I see is a fine, chocolate, 6'3" tall, handsome hunk of a man." Shh, slow my role—Carlos is all that too, Shaymin thought. However, one more before May 8 is not bad.

"Yeah whatever," Roché replied.

"Girl, Roché, the party was awesome. I had a wonderful time as usual. Just as always, I indulged in too many drinks. Right now all I want to do is party, party, party and get my groove on with Carlos every now and then, but I drink too much and end up sick and hung over the next morning. I have to stop doing this. I always start begging God to let me get through it and I won't do it again. I just lie every time, because I go right back and do the same thing all over again."

"Yeah, you are right Shay, because it is only by the grace of God that you are still alive. Because a stunt like you pulled, last night could have been tragedy. Thank God Roger is a good person and got you home safe and untouched." Roché paused then asked, "So what happened last night?"

"I do not know," Shaymin answered shamefully. "Roger said he gave me the time of my life. However, I do not remember anything. We are going out to breakfast; maybe he will elaborate on what actually happened last night."

As Roché poured coffee for both of them, she said, "All I remember is you were having a damn good time, yelling and dancing all nasty as usual, rolling, shaking, and squatting like you always do it. You were yelling 'Party over here! Party over here!' and then I did not hear or see you anymore. I thought well, maybe you were okay to drive home. I didn't know you were luring Roger into your car and home," she laughed.

"That's not funny," Shaymin said.

"Truly, it is not. It is sad and you need to think about not getting so blasted every time you go to a party. Ashley and I always make sure you get home unharmed, but this time you snuck out without telling anyone. Apparently, you had another agenda in mind and it seems as if you got it," Roché pointed her index finger. "Moi has another agenda. Roger! Roger! Roger! Yes, yes, yes. Ha, ha, ha," she laughed aloud.

"Shaymin baby, are you ready to go?" Roger asked as he stood in the doorway of the kitchen and dining room.

"Yes we can leave now. I am hungry," Shaymin replied.

Shaymin ran upstairs to kiss the girls. Blessing and Amen ran and gave their Auntie Shay a hug and a kiss. Shaymin told them, "I will come back later today or tomorrow and take my favorite nieces out for some ice cream. How about that?"

"Okay," they said in unison. "We love you Auntie Shay. Good-bye Auntie."

Roger escorted Shaymin to the passenger side of his 540e Mercedes. The car was gold with tan interior. He opened her door then waited for her to sit comfortably before closing the door and walking to the driver's side. He drove toward Atlantis Boulevard and exited onto Marshall Circle and into Tomberstone Village.

Beautiful neighborhood, Shaymin thought.

Roger drove into his driveway and pressed the remote for the garage to open. Inside was a two-door convertible black BMW.

Chapter Three

"ROCHÉ!" Joshua yelled from the entertainment room.

"Yes babe," she answered.

"Come here please," he said.

As Roché entered the entertainment room Joshua gave her a bewildered look. She responded, "I know no evil and I see no evil. You invited Roger—maybe you have some answers. All I know is that when Shaymin woke up this morning, Roger was in her bed. I do not know anything and she does not remember anything, not even seeing him at the party. You know how my girl Shay is, she goes for the gusto, and she does not stop until she is practically finished, drunk, done."

"What's for breakfast?" Joshua whispered in her ear.

Roché gave Joshua a seductive look and said, "I can think of some indigestible breakfast. What do you think babe?"

"Nah," he shook his head. "Not now. How about some smothered chicken and grits?"

"Yeah, some smothered chicken and grits," she mumbled under her breath as she made her way back to the kitchen. All he ever wants is me barefoot, pregnant, and in the kitchen, she thought. Yeah he wants me to have another child, but he has bumped his head. He never wants to do anything with the girls and me; he never wants to go anywhere. However, I am coming out and he will regret he ever stifled me. I did not get married to stay at home and cater to him and the children. I love them very much but I want to experience more than these four walls of this mansion. I have too much in me to be sheltered. I promise myself this is the year for me to make a drastic change. I will be happy. I will have nothing less than happiness for the rest of my life…

"What do you do? What do you do?" Roché questioned herself.

After planning, preparing, hosting, and cleaning up after the party of the season, Roché decided it was time for some "me time." It was the cool of the day and the house was still and quiet—the perfect time to grab a chilled glass of White Z and lay beside the pool.

As she relaxed by the pool listening to the cascading sound of her backyard waterfall coupled with the soothing jazz music from the patio speakers, Roché began to reflect on her life and attempted to answer the question of why she was so unhappy and unfulfilled. She took a sip of wine and began to dissect this question.

Roché had been married to Joshua for twelve years, but about four years into her marriage, she realized that she still longed to contact an old close male friend named Shane Jefferson. She had had deep-rooted feelings for him since she was seventeen years old. She and Shane grew up together, were the best of friends, and attended the same private Christian school.

L. Charmane Pough Chestnut

Shane grew up in a large family of five boys raised by both of his parents. Roché's mother had been killed in an auto accident when Roché was five years old. Her father raised the two girls by himself and made sure they had the best of everything. Shane was two years older than Roché and he treated her like his little sister. They would hang out together, laugh and cut up together until one day something happened. Shane brought Roché home and they sat in Shane's car talking. All of a sudden, there was dead silence in the car, their eyes met, and Shane leaned over and gently kissed Roché on the lips. They were both shocked but knew it felt right. They immediately kissed each other, deeply and passionately. Roché felt her body tingle and saw stars. The next word that parted her lips after the kiss of her life was, "Wow." It was a feeling she had never felt before; it was so overwhelming she wanted to cry. She really did not know where to go from that point. Could this be love at first kiss? It was not the first time she had kissed a man, nor was it the first time she had dated or even fallen in love, but this was different. She did not want to do anything to jeopardize their close friendship, so she did not share any of what she was feeling with Shane. She just played it off, said goodnight, and went into her house. Shane went off to college and never knew Roché's true feelings.

Several years passed and Roché went on with her life, forever longing for but never experiencing the feelings or emotions that she had had when she was with Shane. As she reflected on this relationship now, twelve years into her marriage, she realized that she had missed the opportunity of a lifetime—to be with her soul mate. The love of her life had been right underneath her nose and she did not recognize him. Roché deemed it necessary to be true to herself and let Shane know her true feelings. So she decided to start her own investigation—to locate Shane and rekindle what they once had, or better yet to find out if he shared the same sentiments toward her.

She started at the main source, Shane's parents. They were always fond of her and their home phone number had never changed after all of these years. Roché threw caution into the wind, picked the phone up, and dialed the number.

Shane's father answered the phone, "Hello, Jefferson residence".

Roché replied, "Hello Mr. Jefferson, this is Roché Rawls, Robert Rawls' daughter. Do you remember me?"

Mr. Jefferson quickly responded, "Baby yeah, how have you been doing? You know you were supposed to be my daughter-in-law."

Roché couldn't help but chuckle. She said, "I'm doing just fine, but it's funny you would say that because I haven't spoken to Shane in such a long time. I wanted to see if I could get his telephone number from you."

"Sure hon," Mr. Jefferson replied. "Let me see if Mrs. Jefferson can give that number to you."

Mrs. Jefferson ran to the phone, blurted out the number, and then said, "Shane will be thrilled to hear from you baby."

Roché grinned from ear to ear and said, "Thank you! Have a great day and goodbye."

L. Charmane Pough Chestnut

Chapter Four

"IF ONLY for one night..." Luther Vandross serenaded Roger and Shaymin from the car speakers as they drove down Martin Luther King Parkway.

Roger was taking her to the Manestra Café. He said they had the best brunch buffet he'd ever tasted.

"Oh Luther Vandross... If only for one night," Shaymin sang, "one night, one night yeah, if only for one night. Luther is my favorite male vocalist. He can sing me happy any day," she rattled off with a big grin.

"That is funny, Shaymin," Roger chuckled. "You sang that song to me all last night or at least until you fell out."

"Roger that is not funny. I was not in my right state of mind," Shaymin said softly.

"Ooh baby," Roger said, "you may have not been in your right state of mind, however, you made all of the right moves while in your out-of-body experience. I have no complaints." He laughed as he massaged her hand.

"So what is your favorite dish Shaymin?" Roger asked.

"I like seafood. What about you?" Shaymin asked.

"I like Shaymin," he said while blowing her a kiss.

"C'mon Roger, be for real," she said.

"I am for real." He gazed at her with a seductive look. "I do like Shaymin."

"I know why you like me. You took over my body without my permission last night," Shaymin said in a disgusted tone.

"Shaymin, as I said before, I did not take anything; you forced yourself onto me." He added, "You are the best. You know all the right things to do to make a man feel whole and complete. Can you do the same thing sober, or is it the alcohol that influences you?"

"Roger, I really do not want to talk about this because I am very ashamed of myself."

"Why be ashamed? That is who you are, isn't it?" Roger asked.

"No," she blurted out. "That is how I act under the influence of alcohol. Sober, I am a nice, wholesome young woman, who wants to excel in life, who wants to go places, be adventurous, and explore the finer things in life."

"So can we do a repeat of last night while you are sober?" Roger asked.

"No. I told you I am getting married."

"Sure," Roger said sarcastically.

"Can we please change the subject?"

"Okay, I quit for now," Roger said. He added, "Oh yeah, valet parking. We will do that so you will not have to walk so far. I do not want to tire you out with walking. I can think of many other ways we both can enjoy getting tired," he laughed.

"Is there anything else you would like to talk about other than sex?" Shaymin asked.

"Yes! Our future together," he said with a loud sighed of relief.

As the valet attendant opened Roger's door, Roger whispered to him, "I'll open her door." Roger hurried around to open Shaymin's door, fell on his knees, gazed into her eyes, and said, "Will you marry me?"

Grinning from ear to ear, Shaymin said, "You are silly."

But Shaymin considered his words. It is like love at first sight, she thought. I know he is just kidding, but I really like him. There is some chemistry mixing between the two of us, and from what I have seen of him thus far, my answer may be yes…

As Beverly, their server, approached their table Roger inquired, "What would you like to drink this morning?"

Shaymin, still stunned from his words, was in a daze.

"Shaymin," Roger whispered softly, "what are you drinking this morning?"

Shaymin jumped slightly. "Oh yeah, I will have coffee and water with lemon." Even as she said it she thought, I need another drink to get over this hangover, because all water does, is make me sicker. But, I will be cute this morning and sip on my coffee and water. Oh God, please do not let me get any sicker.

Beverly greeted them, "Good morning, welcome to Manestra Café. Have you ever eaten here before? This is one of the best restaurants in the heart of Las Vegas. What would you like to drink this morning?"

Roger replied, "Please serve my lady coffee and water with lemon, and I'll have a glass of orange juice."

As their server walked away, Roger asked, "Will you be eating from the bar or will you need a menu? They have some great food here. I frequent this place, before work, after work, anytime. My office is four blocks over on H Street. 1536 H Street NW is the address."

Roger began to massage her fingers, "So Shaymin, tell me about yourself. Do you get blasted on a regular basis and invite strange men into your bed?"

"Humph," Shaymin grunted. "Well, blasted, I do tend to get blasted too much, but strange men, no. I am usually not alone. I am always with my friends or my fiancé. Ashley, Roché, and I are usually out together, and they make sure I arrive home safe and alone. They are my best friends; they take very good care of me."

"Why do you drink to get drunk and not just socially?" Roger inquired.

Shaymin lowered her chin into her hand and her watery eyes traveled to his. "I can hide all my problems and frustration and insecurities behind the alcohol. I never feel alone when I am blasted."

"Do you care to elaborate on some of your problems or insecurities?" Roger inquired. "I find it hard to believe you are insecure. You are a beautiful black lady with a well-rounded, attractive body. You sound very intelligent. You have a spectacular home and you are soon to be married to your soul mate."

Shaymin agreed, "Yes, you are right about many things, but soul mate, I don't think so. Anyway, can we talk about me later? I need to know exactly what happened last night."

Chapter Five

BEVERLY sashayed back to Roger and Shaymin with their beverages.

"Attorney Thanksgiving, is that you?" she inquired. "I kept looking at you and wondering how I know you. I just remembered. You represented my brother, Cosmos Johnson, when he killed my uncle in 1980. He shot my uncle Jason Jetson. Uncle Jason was pretty crazy that day, he had death on his mind, he told everyone he saw, 'If I see my wife Eartha today I'm going to kill her.' His eyes were bloodshot. He was destined for death.

"Uncle Jason thought Aunt Eartha was cheating on him, but all along he was the one cheating on her. My brother Cosmos beat him at his own game and shot him down right in our hometown of Northland, Georgia. Thanks to you, Attorney Thanksgiving, Cosmos was acquitted. Once the officers opened the trunk of Uncle Jason's car they found a sawed-off double-barrel shotgun and all of Aunt Eartha's clothes in there.

"He would have blown Aunt Eartha's brains out, had he gotten to his trunk. Thank God Cosmos was there. I like the way it turned out. Jason's dead y'all!" she laugh aloud.

"Ms Johnson," Roger politely interrupted, "can we eat now?"

Beverly chuckled. "I am on duty aren't I? I was just a little carried away for a moment, just reminiscing on the past. I see you are still as fine as you were ten years ago, and I still have a crush on you. Are you still single?" she asked.

"Yes," he said as calmly as he could without raising his voice.

"Hi," Beverly said as she extended her hand to Shaymin. "I am Beverly Johnson. And you are?"

"Shaymin Cumbersome," she said softly.

"Nice to meet you."

"Yes, pleased to meet you too," Shaymin smiled slightly.

"Girl," Beverly started back up again, "Shay you have you a fine one here. Isn't he fine? He was a knockout ten years ago; now he is a technical knockout in round number one. Ooh, I wish—"

"Ms Johnson," Roger said.

"Oh yeah," Beverly blurted out, "I am sorry and I am gone! Can I get you anything else?"

"No thank you," Roger and Shaymin said simultaneously.

As Beverly left, Roger said, "Wow, yes, you can get us something; get us away from you." They both chuckled quietly.

Roger apologized, "I am sorry for our cousin's behavior. You know we all have some of those family members who do not know what to say nor do they know when to say it."

He paused then said, "So Ms. Cumbersome, are you sure you are ready for marriage?"

L. Charmane Pough Chestnut

"Yes," Shaymin said, pasting on a smiled. "My clock is ticking and I need to go on and do this, have my babies and live happily after."

Roger asked, "Do you think it is true that people can live happily ever after?"

Shaymin replied, "I think... I think you can live happily ever after if both parties are willing to work at the marriage 100 percent, not fifty-fifty, but 100 percent from both parties.

"Well Mr. Thanksgiving, why aren't you married yet? You do seem to be an eligible bachelor. Your priorities are in order and you have women like Beverly waiting for at least ten years, on you to ask her for a date. Sounds like you have it going on." She grinned liked a Cheshire cat.

Roger agreed, "Beverly is funny and maybe lots of fun, but since I slept with you last night I have a true desire for more of you. Do you think we can plan a date, maybe the next time your fiancé is out of town?"

"I will think about it Roger," Shaymin replied graciously. "However, I really need to know what you did to me last night."

"Well," Roger said, grinning from ear to ear, "last night was a lot of fun. You were pretty... funny and very... persistent. Fortunately, I am a gentleman and I wouldn't dare stoop so low as to try and love you or romance you while you were in the state that you were in last night. I promise you when it does happen it will be consensual and a lot of fun for both of us. However," Roger continued, "I had to restrain you to keep you off me, and that was no fun." With a sweet, intimate whisper he continued, "I promise you when I do make love to you, whether you are intoxicated or sober, you will remember every minute of it. It will be so good you will wake up yearning for more of me."

Right, Shaymin thought. Carlos said the same things but I have yet to reach ecstasy. I sure would like to yearn for more of Roger. I have made a vow to Carlos that I will become his wife. Nevertheless, one more Roger would not be bad. I think if Carlos had an opportunity like this one, he would jump on it. I hope not, but I think he would.

"Shaymin are you okay?" Roger asked.

"Yes, yes," she said quickly. "I was daydreaming for a moment. I was caught up in your comment about yearning for more of you."

"Yes," he said confidently, "you would remember every moment and yearn for more. I would make every muscle in your body contract and every fiber of every hair on your body stand tall, sending chills down your spine." He chuckled. "Yes, I would make you laugh when there is nothing funny, make you cry tears of joy, and make you say mmm, mmm GOOD, with a capital G-O-O-D."

Beverly made her way back to their table with their beverages. She took their order. "Will you be ordering from the menu or will you have the breakfast bar today?"

"We will be eating from the breakfast bar," Roger replied.

As they strolled around to the breakfast bar, a voice shouted, "Shay!" The woman weaved and bobbed her head and opened her eyes wide. "How are you, and who are you with, and why? Where did you meet him and where is Carlos?"

Shaymin recognized her friend. "Good Lord. Ashley, girl please, one question at a time. And remember I am a grown woman." She turned to Roger. "Roger this is my girl Ashley. She and her husband Harry are here for the same reason we are, to have a delicious brunch. On the other hand, is Harry in the doghouse? Is that the reason he brought you out for brunch this morning?" She continued without waiting for a response. "Roger and I met at the party last night and we arranged to meet for brunch today. Is that okay with you, mother?"

"It is okay with me," Ashley teased her. "The question is, is it okay with Carlos? What would he have to say if he knew you were having brunch with someone you met at a party last night? Ha, tell me, how would he feel if he knew his fiancé was on a date with another man? Please tell me, how would my little innocent Carlos feel?"

"Well Ashley," Shaymin sighed, "this is between you and me, and Carlos does not need to know anything. Furthermore, we are just having brunch. It is not as if I have gone to bed with him or even made any advances at him."

"Huh. Knowing you Shay, you probably took him home with you and no telling what else happened."

"C'mon Ash, you know me better than that," Shaymin said as she extended her engagement ring in Ashley's face. "Remember, May 8 I'll become Mrs. Shaymin Butler. There is no way I am going to change my mind. I love Carlos sooo much."

"Yeah, you are right I know you, that is why I am concerned that you are on a date with someone other than Carlos. Furthermore, girl, that ring is just an outward expression of what you want...but what is truly in your heart?" Ashley asked.

"Okay Ashley," Shaymin said sarcastically, "let just discuss this later. By the way, where is Ava?"

"Ava is with her grandma Girtee this weekend," Ashley

answered. "Grandma babysat so we could enjoy the party last. I am sure you had a good time, because you stayed on the dance floor all night long, dropping it like it's hot and backing it up and rolling it around and doing it all over again."

"Okay Ashley that is what I do. I thrive on having fun. As for now, I am going to enjoy my brunch with Roger and you should do the same with Harry. Yeah, yeah, I know what you are thinking. I need to get saved and need to be in church on Sunday."

"Ciao," they said in unison.

Chapter Six

"ASHLEY is pretty darn funny," Roger said, "and she asks many questions doesn't she?"

"Yes, she has many questions and many answers and some type of experience with every subject. I call her newscaster Reese. She is my girl and I love her to death, but she has her issues also, just as we all do. But I know I have issues and I do not try to fake the funk, but she, or should I say they, the Reeses, have many issues and they are Christians and act as if they don't have anything wrong with them. She does not work; she home schools their daughter Ava.

"Harry owns and manages Reese's Mane & Tail Men's Grooming Salon. It is located on 1700 Gervai. He has the entire block locked down with his booming business. They have many high-class men coming through and women who come seeking Harry—oops, I mean seeking men." Shaymin laughed as she finished. "Sometimes the friends they hang with make you think they have forgotten who they are and where they came from. Anyway, to each his own."

"You know Shay; I have been in that salon before, but just for a haircut. I do not recall seeing Harry," Roger replied.

"No! He probably was in the back getting his groove on. They do have beds in the back, where women of their choice can massage the men. He has three female employees that can *really* use their hands if you know what I mean... I mean really use their hands in the right way for a man to keep coming back for more and more," Shaymin explained.

"Okay, enough of Ashley and Harry, we were supposed to be discussing us, and our future," Roger smirked.

Shaymin smiled and said, "You are crazy."

As Carlos left his third meeting, he stopped to call Shaymin. The phone rang and rang, and then Shaymin's answering machine picked up. "Hello, you have reached Shay's pad. Please leave a message after the beep. Thank you and have a great day."

Where could my baby be? Carlos thought. I know the party was last night and she probably had a hangover. Oh tag, maybe she is still sleeping or in the shower. He said into his phone, "Hi baby, this is Carlos, just wanted to call you and tell you how much I love and miss you. I look forward to seeing you on Tuesday. I will call you later sweetie."

Carlos began to think, I really do love Shaymin; she is the love of my life. I will give her the world and anything I have she can share with me. I have never been so in love in my life, but I am afraid she may not feel the same about me. I know she accepted my proposal and said she would become my wife, but I am very apprehensive as to whether she really loves me or just loves what I do for her. She used to be more attentive to me than she is now; she seems to be more preoccupied with her work and partying and drinking more and more. I have tried talking to her, but all she ever says is, "I am okay." I will initiate another conversation about us when I get back home on Tuesday. I will continue to lavish her with silver and gold and anything her heart desires, because she is my pride and joy, the love of my life. I would give my life for her.

Carlos decided to do his traditional thing, go shopping for Shaymin. He would not dare go home without buying something. As he drove his 2004 Lexus to the mall, he decided upon a tennis bracelet for Shaymin. He entered Marshall's Diamond and Jeweler.

"Good afternoon," the jeweler, whose nametag said "Tom," greeted Carlos. "How may I help you today?"

"I am looking for one of the most beautiful tennis bracelets you have in the showcase; it's for the greatest woman in my life, my fiancée. She deserves nothing but the best quality in everything that she owns. I will settle for nothing but the best for her," he chuckled gently.

"Sure," Tom said as he pointed Carlos toward the tennis bracelet display. "You chose the best time to come. We have a great sale today—50 percent off. I have a two-thousand-dollar two-carat bracelet that is on sale for half-price, how does that sound?"

"That is great by me," Carlos responded. "Oh, that is beautiful and it looks like an appropriate bracelet for her—it will complement her well."

Tom seemed excited about the sale. "Is there anything else I can show you today? Would you like to look at some matching earrings today?"

"No thank you, but can you put it in a nice gift box for me, please? She is going to be ecstatic."

While traveling back to his hotel, the Dandridge Marks Hotel and Suites, Shaymin was in the forefront of Carlos' mind. I really wonder where Shaymin is, he thought. I will check my messages to see if she has called once I get back to my room. I am so glad I have chosen her to be my wife. I know with me she will never need or want for anything. I want to make up for all the hurt she has experienced in the past. I do not want her to hurt again, not ever... G&G's trucking, the company my father and I built, has really expanded and made me happy and rich in less than five years. All I lack now is Shaymin as my wife, and that is due to become reality on May 8 of next year, thank God.

He checked his messages and found there were not any. Oh well, I am sure she will call me tonight, he thought.

Carlos decided to have a drink. He knew it would not eliminate his problems, but it would make him forget them for now. Tom, oh Tom, the thought of that name made him sick to his stomach.

He sat on the side of the bed thinking about Shaymin. All I ever wanted to do was to succeed in business and in love, and take care of my family. I will be getting married next year unless Shaymin finds out about the secrets I have been storing in my closet. I can still remember how alienated I felt from my family after Uncle Tom molested me.

Uncle Tom was my favorite uncle, until one night he came to our house drunk as a skunk and fell asleep in my bed. It was about two o'clock in the morning. A hand massaging my back awakened me, and then I heard Uncle Tom say, "Do not say a word or I will kill you and your mother." Oh, this was the most horrifying experience I have ever had; all I could think about was how it hurt, and it really did hurt. Once he finished he just politely got up and left as if nothing ever happened.

To this day, neither Uncle Tom nor I have said anything to anyone. That was the most horrific feeling I have had in my life. However, since then I have been in this compromising position again with Henry, and it was a much better experience, in fact, I rather enjoyed it. Nevertheless, I must let the past be the past and move on with my life. Umm, I can never let Shaymin know about this chapter in my life. She would never forgive me. We have discussed several topics and reminisced about our past, but not once have I told her about my other lifestyle. I promised myself I would never let this or me come out of the closet. I will take this one to my grave...Yes! Take it to my grave.

By now, Carlos had had his third shot of Remy Martin and he was feeling really good. He was having that unusual feeling—yes that feeling, that desire that only Henry could fulfill. Well, he thought, I have promised myself that this chapter in my life is finished, completed. I must convince myself that it is over.

Chapter Seven

"HARRY, guess who I just saw without her fiancé, Carlos, but with another man?" As Ashley spoke, a thread of jealously wove its way though her body. She thought, Shaymin always finds some really handsome and fine man. Oh my, how I wish—oh God forgive me for lusting after what's not mine and learn to appreciate what you have given me. It's just that what you have given me no longer thrills me. I have no desire to touch or feel Harry anymore. Lord, I pray, help me to be fulfilled in you and in my marriage.

"Oh yeah Harry, I apologize, I was in a daze. I saw Shaymin and some guy named Roger she met at the party last night. She said they made plans to meet here for brunch today. Knowing her, she took him home and slept with him last night. That girl needs to get her act together."

"Ashley," Harry laughed, "listen who is talking. As holy as you claim to be, you are always running and shouting around the church, like you are crazy, always getting your dance on. You need to get your act together; you need to sweep around your own front door before you look for trash at someone else's door. You are always finding something wrong with someone else. Shaymin is a single young lady. She can have male friends if she wants and as many as she likes. So what," he said with a frustrated look, "are you jealous? Do you want some male friends like those that Shaymin always finds? Are you not happy in your current situation? Just because you see, her out to brunch with someone other than Carlos does not mean she is sleeping with him. Is that what kind of friends you hang around with? You know what the old folks always say; birds of a feather flock together.

"What type of friend are you? You are always talking about Shaymin and how she runs her business, how she always gets drunk and falls out and how Roché just stays up in that house and cooks and slaves for Joshua and the girls. What does Ashley do wrong? Nothing! Ha, have you ever thought about not talking about them and praying to God for them instead? Is that not what you should be doing? Just maybe if you were tending to your own business I would..." He stopped quickly and lowered his head.

"You would what?" Ashley asked harshly.

"I would come home earlier every night. Instead, I intentionally wait until I think you are asleep before I come home. You can be such a nag. Every time you open your mouth, something negative always comes out about me. You say I never do anything right. Your main saying is nobody wants me," Harry laughed aloud. "You know the Word of God says it is better to be on the rooftop of the house than to be in the house with a nagging wife. Therefore, I stay at the salon where there is peace rather than come home to a whole lot of friction and noise."

Ashley angrily replied, "If you spent more time with your family and in church Deacon Reese, maybe, just maybe, I would not have so much to fuss about."

"Yes, you are right," Harry said, "maybe you would not fuss so much; I sure wish you did not. I provide for you and Ava and I have never asked you to work on anybody's job. You can go shopping anytime you want to. I have never complained. You are never satisfied; you are the most insatiable person I have ever known. I am very confused about how to please you anymore. You have always wanted to live large; here we own our own home in the Marietta's Estates. You have everything you have ever desired in a home, and a brand-new 400 series BMW. What else can a man give his wife to make her happy? Can you answer that for me? Please! The Word of God says a sanctified wife will make a sanctified man. Maybe if you practice at home what you preach in church we both would sanctify ourselves holy."

After such a harsh response from Harry, they ate the rest of their brunch in total silence.

"So Shaymin, how is your meal?" Roger asked. "I hope my choice of restaurant was pleasing to you. As I stated before, I frequent this place because the food and service is usually really great. I think our overly friendly server is new here. I have never seen her here before."

"Roger," Shaymin sighed, "you could not have chosen a better place to dine. The food is absolutely delicious and I have enjoyed every moment I have spent with you. I do appreciate how polite you have been."

"So Shaymin baby, what are your plans for the rest of the day, for tomorrow, or next week? I would like to spend some more time with you." Roger continued, "Outside of being a little out of character last evening, I truly think you are a very classy young woman. I would love to get to know that true loving person who is hiding on the inside. I know you said you have some past hurts and failures; we all do. I would like to help you overcome your past hurts. I would love to have the opportunity to hear about what has caused so much agony and pain in your life. I will not be too persistent; I will wait until you are comfortable enough with me to share your innermost feelings and your disappointments."

Shaymin shockingly looked at Roger and said, "Roger, I truly appreciate your behavior last night. I thank God for choosing you to be the person to help me home safely last night and I thank you for being such a man of integrity. I do want to apologize, and say how sorry I am for allowing myself to go to the extreme of inviting you over without even knowing you. Please forgive me."

"No, Shaymin," Roger interrupted, "no apology needed. It was my pleasure to have done what I did last night. I am glad it was I for several reasons. First, I have met such a wonderful young lady whom I look forward to seeing again and again and again," he smiled. "Second, I hope you feel the same and will accept my invitation to go out with me again. Third, I'm glad it was I, and not some knucklehead that could have beaten, raped, or even killed you. Thank God for grace."

Yes, Shaymin thought, I truly thank God for grace and mercy. I could have been a statistic. To Roger she said, "I promised my girls Blessing and Amen I would take them out for ice cream today. Would you like to join us?"

L. Charmane Pough Chestnut

Chapter Eight

THE SUN was very hot as Ashley sat on her deck and looked over her and her husband's estate.

When did things start falling apart between her and Harry? She took a sip from her espresso latté, thought about the good times, and wondered how they could bring those good times back.

Harry had fulfilled his dream of building a multimillion-dollar salon empire in less than four years. Ashley had gone to school and gotten her Bachelor of Science in Child and Family Studies, her Masters in Education, and her PhD in Child and Family Psychology. However, she chose to stay home with Ava so that Ava could have the full attention of at least one parent. Ashley was still puzzled about why Harry was in such agreement with her decision to home school Ava. Could it have been he wanted her busy, too busy to check to see what he was doing? On the other hand, could it have been he knew what was best for Ava? Sometimes she still wondered why he pushed so hard for her to stay at home.

Ashley stood with her espresso in her hand. She thought it would be nice to take a walk around the garden to clear her head. As she started down the steps she still could not get the conversation between her and Harry out of her head. She thought that they were past that point in their marriage where they were still looking at each other's faults. Even when Harry cheated on her, she worked through it. If anything, she could have held it over his head, but even through that ordeal, she trusted God and believed everything was going to be all right. It seemed as if every time she said anything about her girls, Roché and Shaymin, Harry put up a defense and made her feel as if she were the worst person in the world. Nevertheless, they were her girlfriends, and what she said to Harry was nothing short of what she would say to them. Even in her thoughts, Ashley began to be suspicious of Harry.

As she walked through rows of lilies and the spread of wild-flowers, the scent of each flower continued to push memories forth. She remembered when she and Harry needed time apart; it was hard, but in that separation, she found true love. Yes, love in an extraordinary way. Ashley was thinking of none other than Keegan Hodges. Keegan was everything Ashley wanted and needed in a man. He was warm, caring, and always willing to listen to Ashley. They both had the same dreams and outlook on life. He was also interested in education. He had his PhD in Psychology as well, but his main research and concern was the unity of marriage, with a focus on how a man should treat a woman.

Ashley could still remember the first time she saw him. She had come to a convention on educating parents about schools and their children. Although she did not work anymore, she still received mail from the Psychological Association. Since Ashley had nothing else on her agenda, and Ava was out of town with some friends, she decided to attend the convention; it was in Waikiki, Hawaii.

When she stepped into the Biltmore Hotel, she saw him. Keegan was sitting at the bar alone. She was thirsty from her ride from the airport, so she decided to go to the bar for a drink. As she sat down Keegan looked her way and their eyes locked! Abruptly Ashley looked away, came back to her senses, and ordered her drink.

Just when she was about to go to her room Keegan came over.

"Hello, my name is Keegan Hodges. Are you here for the convention?"

"Yes," answered Ashley with butterflies in her stomach. She kept her head down the whole while, too shy to look into this hunk of a man's eyes. She knew what she felt but was not sure what Mr. Look So Good was thinking of her. She had been separated from Harry for over six weeks and she needed the affection of a man badly. It was almost forty-five minutes into the conversation before Ashley finally looked up. His masculine, sexy voice did not do justice to what sat before her. All she could think was, wow!

The week in Hawaii was a life-changing experience. Keegan made her feel like a phenomenal woman. He touched every essence of her being, from every emotion to every fiber of hair and skin. Ashley's favorite moment was when they spent their very last night together in a beautiful resort owned by one of Keegan's friends. He planned everything from the wild cherries to the homemade whip cream. He also managed to get lilies in every color, knowing they were Ashley's favorite flower.

"I wish this would never end," Keegan said on that last night together.

"So do I," replied Ashley. "Nevertheless, we have to get back to reality. I have a child to go home to and you have your life."

Keegan interrupted, "Ashley I love you."

Ashley could not say another word. They kissed passionately for what seemed like hours. As they looked into each other's eyes, Keegan said, "This will be a night you will never forget."

They made love over... and over... and over again. He made sure every inch of Ashley's body was screaming for more.

Ashley snapped back to reality and started back toward the house. How amazing, she thought, that after five years I still remember it all as if it happened yesterday. How I wish I could push the rewind button and play that role all over again. I do still have his number; I just might have to give him a call. Yes, if Harry continues to stay out until the wee hours of the morning, then I will call my tender, loving Keegan so I can get all that I have been missing for such a long, long time.

Suddenly the phone rang. It startled her and it really broke the moment. It was Harry. "What does he want?" Ashley shouted as she realized that she was back to reality.

She thought, I am going to show up at Reese's Mane and Tail on a regular basis to see what is really going on at the salon. I need to know what is really keeping him there until the wee hours of the morning. I know sometimes I am not easy to get along with; I know I have some issues I need to deal with, such as the manipulating spirit I have, the got-to-have-it-my-way spirit, my non-submissive spirit, and most of all my gift of gab. I have to talk and talk all the time, or, as Harry said, nag. Lord help me to get myself together. Lord, only you can help me to change and not have the feelings and emotions that Keegan inspire. Keegan really made me feel like every woman desires to feel and should feel. So Lord, I pray that I can have this in Harry and not in someone else's husband, although I know Keegan is my soul mate—yes, my one and only soul mate.

Chapter Nine

"ROCHÉ," Shaymin yelled as she and Roger pulled into Joshua and Roché's driveway. "What's up girl? What are you doing?"

Roché responded somberly, "You know, the same ole, same ole: domestic affairs, yard work, cooking, cleaning, and anything else that pertains to being a homemaker. Sometimes I hate that I ever decided to start my own business in my home, because Joshua forgets that I work also. He thinks because I am at home all day long I just sit around and do nothing. However, all is well. So how was your brunch?"

"Super," Shaymin smiled. "It was deeelicious; we must go there soon. Yes, maybe you will get to meet Roger's secret admirer. The secret is out now. Beverly was very comical. She was our server and before she took our order, I knew her whole life story. Roger defended her brother in a murder trial. Oh yeah, let me tell you something funny, Beverly said Roger was a knockout ten years ago, but he is a technical knockout in the first round now," they laughed in unison.

Shaymin continued, "And child, oh girl, let me tell you, of all people, I ran into our girl Ashley, who gave me the third degree. She played detective, asking all kinds of questions about Roger. She even had the nerve to say I probably took him home and the rest is history."

"Well," Roché said sarcastically.

"Nooooo," Shaymin said slowly, "nothing happened." She smiled. "Roger is a man of integrity. I will tell you later." Shaymin walked toward the door, looked over her shoulder, and winked her eye. "By the way, where are my girls Blessing and Amen? I promised them I would take them out for ice cream today."

"They are upstairs, ready and waiting on Auntie Shay," Roché replied. "Blessing and Amen, Auntie is here," Roché yelled from the bottom of the staircase. "Slow down," she said as the girls raced down the stairs, screaming "Auntie! Auntie Shay!"

"We are ready to go for ice cream, cake, and the park," Amen said.

Shaymin smiled. One day, she thought, I would like to experience these things called marriage and motherhood, but it must be in that order.

As Shaymin and the girls got into Roger's car Amen asked, "Auntie Shay where is Uncle Carlos? Who is this man and why is Uncle Carlos not with us? He normally goes with us to get ice cream."

Shaymin smiled eagerly, "Amen, Uncle Carlos is gone on a business trip. This is Uncle Roger; he is a friend of your daddy. He is a good guy, and he will take very good care of us for Uncle Carlos, okay?"

"Okay Auntie," Amen replied.

"She is funny," Roger said. "She reminds me of Ashley with all of her questions, but that is okay. You were quick on your feet with all the right answers."

At the park, the girls swung on the swings. Shaymin sat on the table and Roger straddled the bench while massaging her feet.

"Shaymin," Roger whispered, "What are you doing Saturday night? Your fiancé does not come back until Tuesday. Can we take in a movie and dinner, or maybe even a really nice jazz club? I know of this romantic jazz club in the vista that serves great food. What do you think? I promise you I will be a gentleman again."

Shaymin smiled but she wanted to jump for joy. "Sure," she answered. "We can do that on Saturday. Will you pick me up or should I meet you there?"

Roger responded, "I will pick you up and take you there."

Shaymin almost melted. She thought, I wish you would literally pick me up in you arms and carry me somewhere, to a place I have never been before—to my pinnacle in bed with you. Yes take me there Roger, take me there.

"Shaymin," Roger said softly, "are you okay?"

"Yes," she replied as she snapped back to her senses. "I often venture off into fantasyland..."

To Blessing and Amen, she called, "Girls, let us get ready to go. It is getting late and Uncle Roger may have some other plans."

Roger did have other plans, plans to take Shaymin to higher heights and deeper depths, to explore her and give her his undivided attention.

Carlos lay in his hotel room. He was really concerned about Shaymin's whereabouts so he decided to call her; he got the answering machine again.

"Shaymin please call me as soon as you get this message. I am concerned about you. I have not heard from you all day. My number here is 718-555-7329. I have a great surprise for you and I cannot wait to see you and lavish you with my love. Talk with you later sweetie. Bye-bye."

Carlos was worried about Shaymin. She wasn't answering her phone and she had not called him back. He decided he would call Roché and ask her to pass by Shay's house to make sure she was okay. He dialed Roché's phone number.

"Hello," Roché answered.

"Hey Roché, this is Carlos. How are you, Joshua, and the girls? I am sorry I missed the party last night, but I know you did it up as usual."

"We are all fine," Roché answered.

"I am concerned about Shaymin. I have not heard from her all day and she is not answering her phone. Do you have any idea where she is?"

"Yes Carlos," Roché responded, "she and the girls have gone out for ice cream."

"Okay good," Carlos said. "As long as she is okay, all is well."

"How is your trip and when will you be returning home?" Roché asked.

"Meetings after meetings," Carlos responded. "But overall it's great here in New York. I wish Shaymin could have accompanied me."

Roché shook her head. "Look Carlos, I will make sure I tell her to call as soon as she returns with the girls."

"Thank you," Carlos said.

"You are welcome," Roché said sheepishly.

"Okay, bye-bye," they said in unison.

Carlos hung the phone up and thought, I am still a little apprehensive. This is not like Shaymin. I wonder what she is thinking; she has never done this before. I usually at least get a call the next day but I have been gone for three days and she has not called yet. Oh well, maybe she has called and just did not leave a message. I hope! She has been a little less talkative lately and a little standoffish. I will give her the benefit of the doubt; maybe she just has cold feet with the wedding date being right around the corner. I wonder why she has not said anything about any wedding arrangements or plans lately. I pray she is not having second thoughts—that would break my heart. I love Shaymin so much.

God, Carlos prayed, please do not let Shaymin change her mind. I do believe I have found the best thing that could ever happen to me. As the Bible says, when a man finds a wife, he finds a good thing and obtains the favor from the Lord. Lord, I know Shaymin is my good thing and I truly want to make her my wife. Please let nothing or no one set us asunder. Thank you, in Jesus' name, Amen.

Chapter Ten

AS SHAYMIN drove home she thought, today has been the day of a lifetime. I met a very interesting man. He seems to be just what I have been dreaming of having in my life. I know I am engaged, but Roger has made me think twice about my future with Carlos. I do like Carlos, however, I am not in love with him, and I do not want to make such a great mistake and regret it later. Roger told Beverly he is single, but maybe he just said that to throw me off or better yet, to keep Beverly off him. Whatever the reason may be, I hope he is single. I really like what I see in Roger, although I do not know him well. He is a friend of Joshua and Jody's, so he cannot be all-bad. He didn't take advantage of me last night, so there is some uniqueness about him. I truly look forward to going out with him on Saturday. I hope I will contain myself and not make such a fool out of myself as I did last night.

"Oh my God," Roger sighed as he entered his house. Shaymin, Shaymin, Shaymin, he thought. I really, really like Shaymin. But what do I do? What do I do when what I have in my hand does not look like what is in my head? How do I tell her I am married? I know she thinks I am single—she heard me tell Beverly I was single. Maybe I will just wait until she gets married to reveal the truth to her. She is engaged to be married and I am entrapped in a marriage that I am not happy in. I have not been happy for the last five years. I truly love my son, Roger Tyrone Thanksgiving, Jr. He is my heartbeat. I would do anything to keep him happy. RJ loves his mother—they are inseparable—so I cannot take him and go. I suppose I will just have to stay around for the sake of our son, RJ.

Aw, and not to mention Marcella is pregnant again. I really feel no connection with this child and I really do not think the little girl is mine. Nevertheless, I will do what I have to do in order to keep RJ and his sister together, but I will get a DNA test to find out the truth. Marcella has really damaged my heart with all of her affairs. I know I have not done everything right, and I have caused some hurt in our marriage, but to have someone cheat on you as many times, as she has cheated on me has really messed me up emotionally. Man, has she cheated on me. She has cheated on me several times—several times—and I took her back each time. I feel like the man in the Bible, I think his name was Hosea, whose wife Gomer was a prostitute.

Why, oh why did I marry Marcella? Because I thought, she was the woman for me. I knew she was not ready to settle down; she had not finished sowing her wild oats yet. I thought that I was in love, but I now realize that I wanted to break the generational curse. It was the thing for all the men in my family to divorce their wives and I really did not want to be a statistic. I wanted to be married for life. Oh, how wrong I was and how miserable I am now. I should change my name to Hosea. Get it—"whore-sea." The whore was saved by me, because, the average man would have beaten her brains out and treated her as a whore. Oh no, I tried to do the right thing and love her as a wife and treat her as a wife should be treated. What thanks did I get in return? Yeah, a whole bunch of hell as if I were the bad person... As matter of fact, I still ended up being a statistic anyhow. Just for the record, I ended up being a damn fool for staying with such a b----.

Consequently, I would think because of all the hell she has put me through that she would be eating out of my hands. Instead, she thinks I owe her something; she does not give me credit for anything I do. I cook, I clean, I bring home the bread, and I pay all of the bills. What she does with her money is a mystery. She never has any money or anything else to show for the check that she claims she receives biweekly. I am so glad she has gone to her parents' for the next two weeks. She asked me to go with her and I told her, "Hell no!" I hope that in that time I can get to know Shaymin better. Oh yes, who knows, maybe she will become the next Mrs. Thanksgiving. I have made up my mind that Marcella and I will not be together much longer.

I really like Shaymin a lot. She is beautiful and I feel like it was love at first sight. Although when I met her she was stone drunk, there was something about her, which really had me curious and it made me want to get to know her inner being. Yes, she does have some problems and some issues, as we all do, but I think we can get to the root of them and work them out together. Yeah, but, right now Marcella is my problem. I know I cannot just up and leave her because the courts would charge me with abandonment and I cannot see paying her alimony and child support. I will just wait her out. Eventually she will get tired of me not caring about her feelings and she will just up and leave. I do not mind taking care of my kids. However, I cannot pay her alimony too, I just cannot.

I think I really deserve someone like Shaymin—someone who can appreciate me for who I am and not just for what I do. Actually, Marcella does not even appreciate what I do; she just complains about everything.

Right now, Roger thought as he settled onto the couch, I am going to have a glass of wine, listen to a little jazz, and think and dream about Shaymin all night long. I find her really striking. Just looking in her eyes sent chills down my spine and made me want to take her off into the sunset and love her being forever and ever...

Carlos answered the phone on the first ring.

"Hello sweetheart," Shaymin excitedly said. "How have you been? I miss you. Did all of your meetings go well? Oh yeah, what surprise do you have for me this time, honey?"

"Shaymin baby, how are you and where have you been? I have tried calling you several times, all I have gotten is your answering machine, and your cell phone went to voicemail. I called Roché and she said you were out with the girls. Is everything okay?"

"All is well," Shaymin stalled, grinning from ear to ear. She was thinking of Roger. "All is well..." she repeated. "I was hung over this morning. As usual, I slept late and then I finally got up and took the girls out for ice cream. Oh, and Amen asked about you. She really wanted you to be there with us, but I took good care of her. But you owe her an ice cream date."

L. Charmane Pough Chestnut

"Well, baby I cannot wait to see you Tuesday and I have a great surprise for you. I will not tell you; I will let it talk to you on Tuesday. Better yet," Carlos anxiously said, "why don't you fly out to see me tomorrow and we can go out on the town on Saturday and Sunday. Your business is not open on Monday and I will have you back early Tuesday so that you won't miss any of your appointments. Baby, please..." Carlos begged.

"Honey I really do not feel like taking a flight out tomorrow. Furthermore, Roché, Ashley, and I are going out for dinner on Saturday," she lied quickly. Carlos must have bumped his head, she thought, because I will not miss my date with Roger for nothing, not even for him.

"Okay baby," Carlos replied, I will let you slide this time since it was such short notice, but the next time we can plan something together. Shay, baby, you are quiet. Did you hear me?"

"Oh yeah," Shaymin replied, still in a daze about Roger. "Yes, I heard you. Anyway sweetheart, Blessing and Amen have really tired me out. I will give you a call tomorrow once I get home from shopping."

"Alright, Shay baby, I love you," Carlos said.

"Carlos, I love you too sweetheart. Goodnight," Shaymin replied.

Chapter Eleven

SHAYMIN looked forward to her date with Roger. She felt excited and nervous and expected a great night.

"Oh what a night," she began to sing. Oh, why am I so nervous? She asked herself. This is not the first date I have ever had. Could it be the first right one? I do feel rather different about this man Roger. Well, it will probably be another catastrophe just as all of the others have been. Whatever the outcome, I will concentrate on having a good time tonight.

Shaymin decided to wear a black, spaghetti-strap, flare-tail sequined dress, with her diamond-cut sequin and black necklace, earrings, and matching bangle. Her shoes also complemented her dress. They were beautiful pumps with three-inch spiked heels and sequins across the toe. They accented her freshly pedicured feet and her French-manicured toes and fingernails. She had had Kim from the salon style her hair in a beautiful updo and her skin was glowing with the final additions of her natural earth-tone makeup.

Shaymin took a step back and took a second look at herself

in the mirror; she spun around and said, "Wow! I look and feel so good I could have a date with myself. I do not know whether my mother and father had a good time or if it was their worst night ever, but fortunately, the night I was conceived they broke the mold. I was and still am the most beautiful thing they ever created. I am pretty. Yes, I am pretty," she said as she admired herself in the mirror. "Why is it that I never meet a man who will love me for who I am and not for what is beneath my clothing?

"Shaymin," she called her name aloud, "snap back to where you are now, and do not spoil this night with all your inner inhibitions. Yes, yes, this night and the rest of my future is going to be great with Mr. Roger Thanksgiving. I sure hope my attire will cause Mr. Roger to want to carry me out again… and again… because damn I look good, I must say so myself."

Shaymin had decided she would get dressed a little early so she would have time to settle down before Roger arrived to pick her up. While she sat down to wait on Roger, she turned on the television. She heard a message from Bishop David J. Banks, a very renowned speaker who could say a word that would not only strike your curiosity but would also sound as if God Himself were speaking directly to you and your situation.

The Bishop began to preach, "Yes, I look good, I am all dressed up and all shook up and all stirred up and all tangled up. Sometimes I am up and other times I am down. I wonder if he is mine or wonder if he will ever be mine. Just a big ball of confusion, I want to feel accepted; I want someone to appreciate me. I need affirmation, but all I ever get is a slap in the face. I work hard everyday and find myself still not satisfied. I drink until I am silly and do not even know my name. I sleep with this man and try another one. Old wretched man am I, who can save me from myself? Jesus says he can save me from myself. The Lord knows the plans He has for you, plans to help you and not to harm you, to bring you to an expected end and a happy ending."

Shaymin quickly changed the channel and made a mental note that maybe she would come back and watch this again. This cable network allowed you to recall any show and play it again. She wrote down the time and the date and set it beside the remote.

Old wretched man am I, she thought, who can save me from myself? God why do I do the things that I do? Why am I so eager to get drunk and not remember the rest of the night? Why, God, why?

Suddenly the doorbell rang and Shaymin snapped back to the reality of where she was and why she was there. "Oh," she said, "Roger is here."

Roger stared at Shaymin with his lips slightly parted and a glare of surprise on his face. "Wow," he said, "you are stunning. My night has already been graced by looking at this live, beautiful, gorgeous, picturesque woman poised in front of me."

With a bashful grin on her face, Shaymin said, "Thank you so much. Please come in while I grab my purse."

Roger stepped inside the foyer with his hand behind his back. He slowly brought his right hand around to reveal a vase containing three roses: one yellow, one peach, and one white. His left hand gently pulled a white envelope from his pocket.

"Oh, my," Shaymin sighed, "you didn't have to do this, but... thank you so much! Should I read the card now?"

Roger answered, "Please do, and yes I do have to do this. It is indeed my pleasure and I am honored to have the opportunity to escort such a graceful and elegant young lady on this night and hopefully future nights as well." He took her hand, raised it to his mouth, and said, "My Nubian queen, thank you!" Then he placed a soft long kiss on her hand as he gazed into her eyes.

Shaymin anxiously, but slowly, opened the card. Roger had chosen a blank card and had handwritten his own message:

The Rose in Your Hand

The Rose in your hand is
Symbolic of who you
Are to me.
Although I've only known you for a short while,
You have shown me with whom
I want to be.

The Yellow Rose symbolizes
The brightness I see when I look into your eyes,
A light shown so bright it causes me to look
Beyond the skies.

The Peach Rose—
The peach oh how sweet.
The warmth from your heart
Makes me never want to part.

The White Rose—
Oh yeah, the pureness of your soul.
And yes it's with you I will love to grow old.

One for the Father,
One for the Son,
And one for the Holy Ghost.
All three make one:
THE TRINITY

For it is in the trinity
And in you I find my true IDENTITY.
Oh, how I long
To spend with you
My joyous and fun filled DESTINY

I applaud you
And tall I stand
For this is how my heart describes
The Rose in Your Hand!

Shaymin blinked her eyes quickly to hold back the tears. She looked at Roger and almost melted as he gently placed his arms around her and pulled her to him. He placed a kiss on her forehead and then on her nose and said, "Sweetheart I don't know why, but what I feel I have never felt before and what I feel is all so real."

Shaymin, at a loss for words, just cleared her throat as her eyes traveled to Roger. She and Roger stood and just gazed into each other's eyes for a short while.

Then Roger abruptly asked, "Oh Shaymin baby, are you ready to go?"

As she caught her breath, she quickly said, "Yes Roger we can leave now."

Chapter Twelve

SHAYMIN still felt baffled by what had just taken place. She sat quietly as Roger drove. Gladys Knight sang over the speakers, "Ain't nothing like the real thing baby. Ain't nothing like the real thing..."

Shaymin felt astonished and didn't know what to think or say. Who is this man Roger? she asked herself. What is his motive? He doesn't even know anything about me, but gives me a handwritten card that blows me away with its heartfelt words. I do like him a lot. What I feel is not sexual expression at all; it is soulful. Could he be my soul mate? Could he be the man of my dreams? Could he be the man I have been longing to have? Could he be, could he be? He has to be married, gay, or crazy, because there cannot be anyone like this in reality; it all has to be a dream or a fantasy... Wake up Shaymin; wake up Shaymin, it has to be a dream.

"Shaymin are you okay?" Roger asked.

His calling her actually startled her because she was truly in a trance. "Yes," she said softly. "Yes, I am okay. I was just taken by all you have done thus far. I am really amazed. I have never met anyone like you, someone who doesn't have an ulterior motive."

"Well Shaymin, I do have an ulterior motive. It may not be in the same essence that you would normally think, but yes, I do have one. Remember 'The Rose in Your Hand.' It describes the true aroma of what I felt the moment I first laid eyes on you. Although you were highly inebriated, and that is okay, when I first saw you, it felt like love at first sight. Yes, love at first sight! What I felt when I saw you, words cannot express. It can only be exemplified through my actions. However, not all that I will to do to you and do for you can be fulfilled at this time. Nevertheless, I promise you, it will be, yes it will…"

Shaymin was still in awe as Roger opened the door and gently took her hand to assist her out of the car.

"The Rostra Cuisine," Shaymin read the sign aloud.

"Yes, my dear, this is one of my favorite spots," Roger replied. "They have Jazz and Calypso. They serve a combination of Caribbean and American food. I hope this is pleasing to your taste."

"Yes, I love Jazz and Calypso and I really love Caribbean dishes, curry, pilaf, roti, et cetera. I can go on and on, because they are some of my favorite foods."

"Oh, I am so glad that we have so much in common. I am so glad that you allowed me to take you out tonight. I am so glad that I met you. I am so glad… I can tell you of so many more reasons why I am glad about July 5, but I don't want to bore you or scare you away," Roger whispered in Shaymin's ear.

L. Charmane Pough Chestnut

Roger requested a seat in the back of the restaurant so that there would be no distractions. He wanted Shaymin's undivided attention, because he wanted this night to be well spent. He wanted to be engrafted with her presence, her aroma, and her entire being.

Shaymin bobbed her head to the soothing jazz sounds cascading from the live band that was performing.

"May I have this dance, my love?" Roger asked as he massaged her hand and gently kissed her earlobe. He stood up and extended his hand to escort her to the dance floor.

Shaymin's heart began to pound, and then it beat faster and faster as he placed his arms around her waist and gently pulled her to him. She placed her arms around his neck and they began to slow dance. Oh, Shaymin thought, what is he doing to me? I cannot seem to handle any more of this. Roger kissed her forehead and then her cheek, and then placed a soft kiss on her earlobe. Shaymin silently mouthed, "Oh my God," as she enjoyed the ride. The ride was so intense she could hardly contain herself. She thought; please don't let me mess up. I am so promiscuous and flirtatious, but please don't let me blow my cover this time. But the man feels so good to me that I just want to explode all over him.

Sandra, their server, arrived at their table as soon as they returned from the dance floor. She asked, "What will you be drinking tonight?"

"I will have White Zinfandel," Shaymin began to speak.

Roger interrupted quickly, "Sweetheart, please let me order for you. May I get a bottle of Dom Pérignon please, so my lady and I can celebrate? I want to celebrate this grand union of us coming together. I have never laid eyes on anyone as beautiful and as classy as you. You make my heart sing, so allow me to celebrate you, right now and for always." While he spoke he massaged Shaymin's hand and enjoyed the beautiful aroma of being in her presence.

Sandra returned to the table with a glass of White Zinfandel, water with lemon, and a bottle of Dom Pérignon, along with two empty champagne glasses. Roger poured some champagne in both glasses, and placed one of the glasses in Shaymin's hand and began to speak. "Shaymin Cumbersome, I know my actions may frighten you a little, but my heart cannot stop pouring into you. As I began to write 'The Rose in Your Hand,' my heart began to blossom. I said words that I never thought I would be able to say again. Baby, it is you and your whole being that has just saturated my mind, body, and soul. I desire to have and to behold you for the rest of my life. If I could, I would love to make you my wife. I toast to you and me forever, for always, and for love…"

Shaymin sat in total awe with tears streaming down her face in response to what he had said. She really didn't know how to receive Roger, nor did she know how to respond to Roger. All Shaymin knew was that although Roger didn't know her and she didn't know Roger well, what she felt at this very moment made her feel as if they had been in love for years and she never wanted it to end.

"Roger," Shaymin whispered as she turned slightly toward him and gathered her composure, "I don't know the real meaning of our meeting, but I am just ecstatic. I never believed that there could be love at first sight, but I feel as if we have known each other for many years. I wish this night would never end. You have made me feel as if I were the Queen of England. I have never felt so in tune with a man before. I am really frightened about what I feel and desire. What I feel feels too good to be true."

Roger gently placed his finger on her lips as if to say "shhh." Then he said, "I know baby, I feel the same way too..." He pulled her to him and put his arm around her shoulder. She relaxed in his arms and they enjoyed the rest of the night holding each other, kissing, and swaying to the sounds of the live band.

Chapter Thirteen

Labor Day

ALFONZO, Shaymin's cousin, was having a fiftieth birth-day party and Shaymin was having herself a ball. She was screaming, "Hey! Hey! Hey! Party over here! Party over here!"

A song played loudly over the speakers, "Fire ya, we don't need no water let the mother, mother burn. Ain't gonna hurt nobody to get on down, don't stop me and I won't stop you." But no matter how loud the music, Shaymin's voice could always be heard. She had one of those distinctive voices that was easy to recognize, especially if she had had a few drinks, and that night she already had.

"Alfonzo," Shaymin screamed his name, "tell me what's up? Are we gonna party tonight or what? Please don't let me get too blasted tonight. I am expecting a real special friend of mine to show up at anytime, and you know how I always overdo it. I want to stay conscious tonight and stay on my best behavior."

"Well coz," Alfonzo screamed back, "I can't baby-sit you now. I just suggest you stay away from the bar and stay on the dance floor. You know in a few more drinks I will be wasted and not know who or where I am. It is my fiftieth birthday and you know I am gonna tie one on. Who is this special friend, and where is Carlos?"

"Umm, Roger is a friend I met on July 4 at Joshua and Roché's house party and we have grown very fond of each other over the last couple months. We have shared a lot and have become very good friends. Now, you know I am engaged to marry Carlos next year. By the way, he is gone on another business trip to Seattle, Washington."

"Yeah, yeah, Shay, you say you are getting married next year, but you know how the Cumbersomes and the Carpenters roll—in today, out tomorrow. Anything can manifest between now and then, and there may not be a wedding. As a matter of fact, I am willing to bet my life on it. You will not be getting married, at least not next year and not to Carlos."

"C'mon Alfonzo, you know I won't do that to Carlos. I really love him and he really loves me. And the nerve of you Alfonzo! You have Rockale, your wife, and Roxanne and Angel, your girlfriends, here at the party. How can you be so crazy?"

"Coz, like I said, you know how the Cumbersomes and Carpenters roll—you may be here today and replaced by someone else tomorrow. Girl, seriously I hope you and Carlos make it. However, I doubt that you will make it to the wedding chapel, yet alone make it a lifetime. Furthermore, you need to check out Carlos's agenda and find out why is he out of town so often. Ha, ha, ha," he laughed as he left bobbing his head to "Bad Boy": "Gonna sneak out tonight, gonna slip out my window."

L. Charmane Pough Chestnut

"Hey Ashley," Shaymin said as she saw Harry and Ashley make their way onto the patio. "Mrs Holy Roly, what are you doing here tonight? Doesn't this kind of music offend your ears? You don't listen to secular music anymore do you? How would Pastor Shelton feel if he knew his Deacon and Deaconess Reese were at the party with drinks in hand? God almighty, I know that is soda you are drinking; it could not be anything stronger, or could it? Sike, just kidding, you can drink whatever you like, because y'all know I am gonna have my share and probably someone else's also. Oops, I forgot, I am on a fast tonight. I am fasting alcohol and men tonight," she lied quickly.

"Yeah whatever Shaymin," Ashley responded, "that's what your mouth says, but we know your flesh and that bar are gonna be saying something different in a little while. But I am praying that you keep your word."

"Girl, you are silly! Don't be praying at this party," Shaymin blurted out loud, and then tickled by what she had said, she laughed and danced away from Harry and Ashley.

"That girl sure is silly and really needs Jesus," Ashley mumbled.

"Ashley please don't start tonight; let's enjoy the party. As a matter of fact, can I have this dance?" Harry asked as "Turn off the Lights" played in the background…

"Hey baby," Roger whispered as he eased up behind Shaymin while she lounged near the pool with a glass of Hennessey on the rocks.

Shaymin felt chills all over her body, and she jumped slightly. "Ooh Roger," she said. "I thought you weren't going to make it tonight. What a pleasant surprise. I am so glad you are here and as always, better late than never."

"May I lie next to you?" Roger asked as he held her hand and placed a kiss on it. "I missed you Shay. We haven't talked for at least three weeks. That is too long to be missing you. How have you been?"

"I am doing great. I was looking forward to seeing you tonight, but I wish you could have gotten here a little earlier and I could have introduced you to some of my family. It is too late now. They are either gone or too blasted and wouldn't remember you. It's okay; we will get another chance, won't we?" She asked, expecting a yes.

"Yes, of course we will. Baby I apologize. I was detained at the office. I went in to take care of some pertinent reports for court tomorrow and time just got away from me," he lied quickly. He and Marcella had had an intense argument. He only came to the party because he didn't want to disappoint Shaymin. "Yes, a lot late, but let's not let anything or anybody waste anymore of our time."

Roger wrapped his arms around Shaymin. They both lay on the lounge chairs and enjoyed the sweet melodies of Luther Vandross, "If only for one night…"

"Shaymin!" Carlos yelled.

Shaymin thought she was seeing a ghost as she jumped up and looked into Carlos' face. "Carlos what are you doing here? You are supposed to be in Seattle."

"No, the question is what are you doing here? And who is this beating my time?" Carlos asked angrily.

"He—" she stuttered, "he is just a friend."

"Just a friend! Do you lounge beside a pool all wrapped with all of your friends?" Carlos furiously blurted out.

"Come on Carlos, it is not what you think and it is not even what it looks like." Shaymin tried to ease his mind.

"Well, please tell me what it is and what are you trying to prove," Carlos shouted as he stormed away from the pool, through the garage, to his car, and out of the neighborhood. He drove as fast as his car would safely allow him.

"Shaymin baby, I am sorry, maybe I shouldn't have come," Roger said.

"No, its okay. Carlos is supposed to be in Seattle and he just shows up unannounced. Everything will be okay. I will talk to him tomorrow. Actually, I owe you an apology for putting you in such a compromising position," Shaymin said as she took another sip from her drink. This could be my way out of this ordeal of getting married, she thought. I really don't think I am ready to be married and especially not to Carlos. This hunk before my eyes has made me want to tell Carlos where to get off, or better yet where to go… to hell. Ha, ha.

"Shaymin," Alfonzo blurted out as he stumbled out near the pool, highly inebriated, "what's up girrrl? You, you have to turn in your player card, come on, and give it up. You know the first rule is you can't get caught in the act." He laughed aloud. "I told you, you won't make it to the wedding chapel."

"Oh Alfonzo," Shaymin replied, "I will talk to Carlos tomorrow, and he will be eating out of my hand again…"

"Yeah that's what your mouth says. Stick a fork in you; you are done," Alfonzo said as he fell back on a lounge chair. "And guess what? I am done too… Goodnight."

Chapter Fourteen

AS SHAYMIN relaxed in her Jacuzzi she began to laugh at the discrepancies between her expectations and the disappointing reality. She wondered, why do I continue to settle for less than what I am capable of attaining? I own a booming salon—ALL N 1—, which offers beauty, massage, nail and pedicure, restaurant, boutique, and exercise gym all in one location. I am very thankful. Needless to say, this is where I was supposed to start and not end up. By now, I should have two salons: an elderly day care and a resort with bed and breakfast amenities. So now, I need to refocus and get back on track and get my life in order again. Maybe I need to get back into attending church.

I can always remember my mother saying, "Train up a child in the way that he should go; although he may stray away, he won't stay away." I have really strayed far away from what I was always taught, as a child. It is so much more fun not having to give an account to God. I don't really have to give an account to anyone...

I often think about Harry and Ashley; they are well-known and faithful people in the body of Christ. They hold great titles, but they are so unhappy. Harry has his own thing going on down at the salon, and Ashley, she is so miserable and confused she sometimes doesn't know whether she is coming or going. I have told her she better put Jesus aside for a day or two and get her a man who can make her feel whole again from head to toe. Let the truth be told, Miss Holy Roly probably has someone but will take that secret to her grave because she has an image to uphold and she would never tell me, the sinner, that she got her a man on the side.

Well I don't know what I am going to do. However, I do know that I am tired of the life I am living. There has to be a better and brighter light at the end of the tunnel. I do know that I can't go and stay at the same time. Considering where I am, I know I am complacent, but should I give my life over to Jesus Christ? I don't know, and I am afraid I may not be ready to make that commitment. I really don't want to make that change and not stick to it, or not do the right thing. The bottom line is I don't want to make that declaration and then backslide.

Startled by the ringing phone, Shaymin pressed the receiver to her ear and said in a groggy voice, "Hello?"

"Hello to you too," Carlos said sarcastically. "Are you ready to explain last night to me or should I just assume what I want and just go on with my life. Now Shaymin, you know what I saw last night was not a pretty picture for any man to come in and see his fiancée lying all hug up with another man."

"Well Carlos," Shaymin began to explain, "you don't have to assume anything, because making false accusations or assumptions will only make an *A Sugar-Sugar* out of you and me, so let me explain myself. Yes, what you saw probably was

L. Charmane Pough Chestnut

not a pretty picture; nevertheless, it was not what you assumed. Roger, whom you saw last night, is a very good friend of mine. I met him at Joshua and Roché's party back on July 4. Remember, you were out of town? You were supposed to be out of town this holiday also. I was so inebriated that night. Thank God, he was a good person, and made sure I made it home safely and was not raped or beaten. Maybe you should explain why is it that you always conveniently plan your business trips on or around every holiday weekend. Is it so that you can't be here with me? Or do you have some other ulterior motive or some secret affair going on out of town?"

"Come on Shaymin, don't even try to switch this back on me. You were caught lounging, or should I say lying, with some other man, and not just lying, but hugged up. How's that for a man to come to a party and find his fiancée, who was supposed to be going to the party stag. Now that's what needs to be explained. As I recall, around the weekend of July 4 I tried calling you on several occasions and I could not get in contact with you. Was it because of this Roger, or were you really, where you said you were? If I remember correctly, you said you were hung over all day. Well, that is not abnormal for you. Or were you being sexed up with Roger?"

"Rog—oh shoot, I mean Carlos," Shaymin quickly corrected herself.

"Oh heck no, here you go calling me Roger... He must have been all so good to you."

"Whatever Carlos," Shaymin interrupted, "as I was saying, we are very good friends. Remember, you were supposed to be out of town. I invited him to come to the party. Now that's it in a nutshell."

"Yeah right, and my head screws on and off. Do you think I

was born yesterday and I am just so naïve you can give me any ole story and I am supposed to say, 'Okay Shaymin, baby everything is just peachy,'" Carlos said facetiously. "So Shay, why is it that I have never met your friend? A friend of yours can also be a friend of mine, can't he? On the other hand, is he a friend you never wanted me to find out about?" Carlos was now livid. "What else have the two of you been doing other than being friends? Has he taken you out? Have you slept with him yet? You know, you are pretty easy. In fact, you were very easy for me; three drinks and you were in my bed. Huh Shaymin, what do you have to say about that? You are very quiet; the cat's got your tongue. You are not going to defend yourself?"

"Well Carlos, there is nothing to defend. I have told you who Roger is, and you continue to make more of the story than what it really is. There is nothing I need to add, other than Roger is a friend of mine. That is my story and I shall stick to it, no matter what you think or do. Furthermore, if you want to call it quits, then good riddance... Goodbye Carlos. Call me if and when you want to be civilized. Love you," Shaymin said as she gently hung up the phone.

Shaymin submerged her body deeply into the warmth of the Jacuzzi. She laughed aloud as she thought of what Alfonzo with his drunk self had told her, "Girl you must turn in your player card, because the first rule is you don't get caught in action." Alfonzo is crazy and he has some nerve to talk; he hasn't been faithful since the day he got married. He has been married for fifteen years. Unfortunately, for Rockale, he has cheated at least fourteen of those years. I wonder how many sexually transmitted diseases he has given her. She will probably be okay with it, because she came from a crazy background. She was poverty stricken for all of her child-hood and part of her adult life. So to have a man and the gorgeous home that she has, she must think she has struck it rich, especially considering what she lived like in the past. To each his own; I call it crazy but she probably called it coming out of poverty. She likes! I love it! Seriously speaking, I wouldn't have my crazy cousin, drunk or sober. All of this is all in the bloodline: promiscuity, alcohol, and partying.

Only God can really change us. I don't like it, but I know no other way to make myself happy and forget about all of the disappointments in my life. I wish I could start all over again; I would do so many things differently. Well since I can't, I need to use wisdom from here on out and try to do the right thing.

Chapter Fifteen

SHAYMIN answered the phone on the first ring. She was upset because Carlos had interrupted her quiet and relaxing bathing moment with all his nonsense. "Yes Carlos," she said abruptly into the phone, "what you want this time? Haven't you said enough to hurt me for today or did you think of something else you need to vent about?"

"No baby, this isn't Carlos, this is your knight in shining armor, Roger. How are you? Considering the way you answered the phone, things must not have been smoothed over with Carlos and you."

"Well, yes and no. I am okay, and Carlos, he will be okay. He made me a little upset; he went into my past to make me hurt the way he hurts. You know the cliché—misery loves company. He is miserable because he thinks something is going on between you and me. Therefore, he wants me to feel bad about having you in my life. He reminded me of how easy it was for him to get me into his bed, and he said it probably was the same scenario with you, just as easy for you to get me in your bed."

"Oh baby, I am sorry," Roger said. "You don't deserve that type of treatment, even though what he saw appeared to be much more than it really was. However, it was innocent last night, although our intentions may have been far from innocent."

"Yeah Roger, maybe I do or maybe I don't deserve the treatment. You know what he saw was a little harsh for any man to see. You always know the right things to say; even in my most downtrodden moments, you can say something to make my spirit smile. For that, I say thank you."

"Ah Shaymin, I just do what I feel, and I feel strongly about keeping you smiling, especially in your sad hour. I want you to smile even when it hurts, because a smile is the most beautiful attire that you can wear. Always remember it takes more muscles to frown than to smile. I want you to keep that beautiful, wrinkle-free complexion. So always, remember a smile is contagious and when you can give one you will always receive one. The Bible says it is better to give than to receive. When you smile you, give life and you are a recipient of life for not being selfish with what God has implanted in you to give freely. A merry heart is like good medicine, so sweet to the soul. So always, remember to be a life giver. Smile—it is like a domino effect that goes on and on and on.

"Now Shaymin, on a serious note, do you think you are ready to marry this man Carlos? Because if he likes to see you hurt now, that behavior will continue into your marriage. He needs to love you unconditionally through the thick and the thin. For him to bring up the past is not real love. He needs to learn how to forgive and move on; until he learns to do that, you may need to reconsider getting married. As a husband, he needs to be able to cover you whether you are right or wrong, not make you feel bad about what you have done wrong. None of us gets it right all the time."

"Roger," Shaymin said as tears began to flow down her face, "you know I really don't know whether or not my decision to get married is a good one or the right one. I think I really do love Carlos, and I need to get married. I am thirty-two years old and I would like to have children before I am old and gray. Carlos is a very good man, a great provider, and a hardworking person. I am not sure as to whether I can make that commitment for life. When I do make that commitment, I do not want to be a statistic, or should I say, I don't want that curse to follow me. All of my aunts and uncles are now married to spouse number two or three, and they are not happy in their present circumstances. So how can I be sure if this is the man for me?"

"Shaymin," Roger whispered softly, interrupting her in midstream, "I want to ask you a question. Are you in love with Carlos? Do you think he is your soul mate? Does he make your world go round and round? In other words, does he rock your world? You don't have to answer these questions now, but they are questions you need to use to analyze whether or not you should make this lifetime commitment.

"And first and foremost, I don't think you are saved and neither am I, but I can remember my grandmother always telling me before I make a hasty decision or attempt to make any commitments, I should always get an approval from God. If it doesn't rest well with you, then maybe you shouldn't bind yourself up with a promise you can't keep. Marriage isn't a fly-by-night game—in today and out tomorrow—it is an institution that is ordained by God. In this day and time too many people take marriage for granted; they get married today and get an annulment tomorrow. Sometimes people treat marriage as if it is a piece of clothing; take it home and if it doesn't fit, take it back and exchange it for another one tomorrow. Our divorce rate is higher than the marriage rate these days. Instead of getting married, people just shack up and when they get tired of each other, they move on to the next victim. Our morals are very low.

"Anyway baby, what I mean to say is make sure this is the right person, because I wouldn't want you to be miserable the rest of your life. Don't get married because you are trying to beat your biological clock, but because you know beyond a shadow of a doubt that this person is for you. Y'all hearts beat as one, meaning you are truly on one accord and hold the same goals and morals in high esteem, so that you can excel together. Remember, haste makes waste."

"Thank you so much Roger," Shaymin chimed in. "I will reevaluate why I want to get married, and consider all of the questions you have asked me before I vow to make this commitment, because I do want to stay in it for life. I know of many people who are in marriages because of their kids. They want their kids to grow up with both parents; the kids are getting the short end of the stick. The kids never see their parents displaying any love or affection toward each other. All they ever feel is friction and disagreement. This makes the children malnourished in the love department. Therefore, they begin to act out because of a lack of love and affection being rendered in the home. Their behavior is terrible."

As Shaymin spoke, she realized that she was speaking from her own experience. Her life had been turmoil. Maybe she acted the way she did because of the lack of true and unconditional love shown in her childhood. She felt that when kids grow up in a hostile environment, they later tend to create this same kind of atmosphere for their kids. They don't know how to receive or to give love. They are born into a bad

L. Charmane Pough Chestnut

experience and bad become normal to them. They resent love, and fight against love, because it's not their normal habitat... They don't know how to be happy; they are emotionally distraught and their minds end up in turmoil and they become victims in their own heads.

"Roger, I know I must face reality and make decisions that will correct me for life and not for the quick fix. Thanks again for all the advice. I will consider all that you have shared with me. And if I may ask, why aren't you married yet?"

"Shaymin baby," Roger quickly changed the subject, "we will discuss that later, and I will call you back later. I have a call on the other line, okay baby. I will talk to you later. Goodbye."

Roger hung up the phone. Whew, he thought, I got out of that one quickly. Shaymin was talking about me when she said people stay in their marriages for the kids' sakes. The only reason I am still with Marcella is RJ and our little girl that is on the way. What a fool I was to fall for another pregnancy. I know I should have continued to wear protection; as devious as Marcella is I should have known better than to listen to her lies. She kept telling me that she wanted to feel the real thing. I should have stuck to my plans and not have fallen for her conniving ways.

Well, it is all done and I suppose I must suffer the consequences. I just hope Shaymin doesn't end up in the same situation I have fallen into. I say, "Fall" because I did fall for this. I really didn't see it coming. I really thought Marcella and I were the ideal couple until I was slapped in the face several times with infidelity... When we do separate, I hope I get to meet the next victim. I want to tell him to watch for the snake in the grass. As a matter of fact, I will pay him to take her off or my hands. She plays that role of Ms nice and naïve. Oh, but when she gets you, she will snap like a snapping turtle.... She will transform into a vicious rattlesnake. She is truly a sheep in wolves clothing.

L. Charmane Pough Chestnut

Chapter Sixteen

SHAYMIN stepped out of the Jacuzzi, grabbed her towel, and then rubbed lotion all over her body. As she did, she thought, I wonder what it would be like to have Roger lotion me down, massaging my entire body from head to toe? "Oh well, what a great thought," she said out loud.

Shaymin had decided to chill the rest of the day, maybe call Roché and bring her up to par on the recent happenings at the party and watch some movies while sipping on some White Zinfandel.

The doorbell interrupted her thoughts. Who could be ringing my doorbell? I am not expecting any company. Oh, it's probably some solicitor trying to sell something. If I don't answer then maybe they will disappear soon. Good Lord she said, as the doorbell continued to ring. My goodness, she thought, they are so persistent. They are just holding the doorbell. Let me see who this is.

"What the—" Shaymin yelled.

"Hell is wrong with me," Carlos said, completing her sentence.

"Yes! You are right," Shaymin answered. "What is wrong with you and why are you here? The way you dismissed me this morning, I wasn't expecting to see you anytime soon."

"I know baby and that's why I am here," Carlos responded. "I came to apologize for what I said to you this morning. I was totally upset and hurt. I kept thinking of you lounging with another man. However, I want to say I am sorry and ask you to forgive me so we can go on with our lives and continue our plans for the wedding in May. Can I take you to lunch this afternoon or do you have other plans?"

"Well," Shaymin sighed as she stepped away from the door, "I was planning to just chill, probably watch some movies and sip on some White Zinfandel."

"Great idea," Carlos said as he reached out to hug her. "Do you mind if I join you? I can order some Chinese food or a pizza or whatever you would like to have. Then you and I can talk and get some things out in the open. Maybe I can give you a massage and cater to you, pour some much-needed love into you."

"Get something out in the open," Shaymin said, shrugging her shoulders. "What could we be hiding, or what do we need to get out in the open? Is there something I need to know?"

"Shaymin baby," Carlos called out, "I will go and pick up your favorite entrée from Red Lobster, get you a bottle of White Zinfandel, get me some Heineken, and come back and chill with you. What do you think about that, honey?" He kissed her on the cheek.

"Okay," Shaymin answered, "if that is what you want to do, then that is fine with me."

"Don't be so excited," Carlos said sarcastically. "I will be back soon."

Haste makes waste Shaymin thought. I really don't want to just settle for less than I deserve. I know I am not in love with Carlos. He doesn't make me tick anymore, and furthermore, I could care less if he ever comes back or not. Yeah, I know he will be back shortly. I just hope he doesn't want me to go to bed with him tonight because I am really not feeling him or it. He said something about pouring some much-needed love into me—oh heavens no. Not today, nor tomorrow, not ever again, do I want him to touch me.

Carlos is really a great man, and I think he will make someone else a very good and proud husband, but he is just not for me. I don't want to end up in a marriage where I am not satisfied. I imagine that really is a miserable life. Marriage is supposed to be happily ever after. I don't want to make a hasty decision that I will cry about later. Therefore, I might need to tell him we need to reconsider this marriage thing. And about this marriage thing, statistics say that on average anybody who has been promiscuous and sexually active with numerous partners is less likely to find him—or herself satisfied in a marriage. Could I fall into this category? Why, of course I could. I have been all of the above—both promiscuous and sexually active with numerous partners. So… I probably won't be happy no matter who I marry.

I remember the first time I actually planned to have sex; it was with Clayton Hawkins. Alfonzo, Lacy Jeffers, Clayton, and I went to the movies. After the movie was over Clayton took Alfonzo and Lacy to the skating rink, and then he took me to a secluded area. Unfortunately, this secluded area was on a back road in the woods. Clayton proceeded to take my clothes off and then we moved to the back seat of the car and the rest was history. Clayton was twenty-one and I was sixteen. I really thought I was in love with him, but after he got what he wanted, he told me I was too young for him...

Shaymin laughed aloud and smiled like a Cheshire cat as she thought; now the only person I really want is Roger... But I think he has a hidden agenda. I only have his work number; he has never given me his home number. I don't want to ask him why he hasn't given me his home number because he may think I am intruding or trying to get in his space... Um yes, how I would love to get in his space. I do need to know what his main objective is. If Roger is not married, then why not? Also, why doesn't he have a friend? There is something funny about this situation. He seems to have so much to offer some young lady. Oh how I wish it were me...

Carlos returned with shrimp alfredo for Shaymin and a fried seafood platter for himself. He had Shaymin's favorite, White Zinfandel, and his six pack of Heineken.

"Shaymin," Carlos said, carefully considering his words, "I really want to apologize for my behavior earlier today. However, I must say I was highly indignant after walking in and finding you and Roger lounging by the pool. I didn't know what to think of the scene that was displayed right before my eyes. I know I could have handled it in a different manner, but I was totally out of control. I also said some things that, I should have not said. Unfortunately, in the heat of the moment, sometimes I am not in control of my actions or words."

Shaymin cut him off. "Okay, yeah Carlos." She shook her head from side to side. "I know what you saw was not a pretty sight, but as I told you, we are just good friends. Roger is someone special to talk to and he always gives good advice

L. Charmane Pough Chestnut

on any situation. He has been a wonderful friend and I am very thankful to have him in my life. I want to say I am sorry you had to walk in and see what you saw. Please forgive me."

Carlos said with a pasted-on smile, "Your apology is accepted. Now can we discuss the wedding plans?"

Shaymin quickly changed the subject. "Carlos, explain to me why all of your business trips are scheduled on holiday weekends. Aren't all major businesses closed on weekends and holidays? Is there something I need to know about?"

Carlos felt tongue-tied. "Shaymin, I think we really need to discuss some things that may cause a change in our future."

Shaymin's eyes traveled to Carlos in a wave of surprise, as if to say, "What on earth are you talking about?"

"Well... well," he stuttered, "we have been dating for approximately two and a half years, and I have asked you to marry me. I do love you and I do want your hand in marriage. I want you to be my bride for the rest of my life. However baby, there is something I must tell you. I hope you will understand that I love you with all of my heart and I don't want anything to separate us. Unfortunately, while I was on one of my business trips about two years ago, I got really intoxicated. I was out of control and I ended up unconscious in this woman's bed. She got pregnant and had a little girl. So while on my trips out of town, I stop in to spend time with my daughter. I named her Shaymin Monaé so I would always have a part of you in my life. But I knew if you ever found out, I would be history."

"NO, NO, NO!" Shaymin screamed in disbelief as she pounded Carlos on the chest. "Please tell me you are lying or that this is a dream. This cannot be true! There is no way you could have done this to me! You have had a child since we have been dating and you didn't even bother to tell me. Oh no," Shaymin began to cry, "why have you done this to me? Why, why? Carlos, I hate you. You have not been truthful or faithful to me. You had me believing you were Mr. Goody Two-Shoes but now let the truth be told. Well I sure do appreciate you telling me before I made the final decision to marry you. I have had an ugly gut feeling for some time about marrying you. Now I realize why I had this feeling. Carlos, you are a two-timing dog. Why didn't you tell me about this earlier, preferably before I made all of these arrangements and announcements?"

"Baby, because I never wanted to lose you," Carlos quickly said. "And baby, I say again, I really cannot fathom living without you. Please give me a chance to make this up to you. I love you and I cannot live without you."

"Carlos," Shaymin said as she settled herself and bobbed her head up and down, "please leave now, and do me a favor—forget my name and number, forever…"

L. Charmane Pough Chestnut

Chapter Seventeen

SHAYMIN gulped down three glasses of wine as she sat on the edge of her bed thinking about what had just happened. Well, she thought, I asked and he gave it to me. He actually gave me more than I was expecting. This explains why he always had a business trip on every holiday weekend. I suppose this is business. He has to play daddy. Oh, I wonder, I wonder where the relationship between he and mama lies now. He is probably taking care of business with her also. As my mother frequently used to say, "What's done in the dark will soon be uncovered." I know she didn't mean any good by saying that, because she always thought that I was a terrorist.

Why, why does this always happen to me? The last two jokers I dated cheated on me and one of them had the nerve to say he wasn't cheating even after we tested positive for a STD. Now Carlos, furthermore, I still don't know what is up with Roger. With all of this confusion in my life, I am ready to say, "To hell with all men and the boat they came in on." I cannot continue to get hurt like this; my heart can't take it.

I thought life couldn't be any worse than what I have already gone through, but it seems like the older I get, the more problems I have.

I have lived in an orphanage since I was three years old. I have been in and out of fosters homes. My biological mother, who was strung out on drugs, abandoned me. I was conceived when she was raped. All of this was just not enough torture. One of the caregivers raped me; he was supposed to have been a caregiver. However, he became a caretaker, because he took my virginity. Yes, Mr. Gigi Salmon took my virginity at the tender age of ten years old. He shoved me in the linen closet, ripped my panties off, and shoved himself inside of me. I can remember it just as if it happened yesterday. It was so painful. He placed his hand over my mouth, held my hands behind my back, and told me if I screamed he would kill me. He did what he had to do, and then left me in the closet to practically bleed to death. Mrs. Ginger Knuckles came to my rescue and took me to the medical unit where I was treated and released. Shaymin wiped the tears from her face and continued to reminisce.

I was pretty much ostracized by my adoptive parents. My adoptive father molested me; he molested me from the age of twelve to sixteen. I never told anyone except my adoptive mother, but of course, she didn't believe me. She would say, "You are just hot in the butt. Whatever happens to you, you deserve it because you bring it on yourself." Ooh, I hated her too. I finally told that bastard, my father, that if he ever touched me again I would kill him. Needless to say, he put me out. I was homeless until I landed a job at McDonalds and was then able to afford my one-room home for twenty-five dollars a week. Oh, thank you Jesus, I had my own place and nobody could ever hurt me again. At least that's what I thought, until now.

L. Charmane Pough Chestnut

What other mishap can I have in life? I am damn near dead now. I was near death's door when John brutally raped and beat me while in college. As my mother said, it probably was my fault, because I was drunk and caught a ride back to the dorm. It was someone who I thought was a friend. I was taken advantage of. I ended up in the hospital with fractured ribs, a fractured jawbone, and a black eye. John Hensen did that to me. He wrote a suicide letter and then killed himself that same night. The letter said:

Shaymin,

I am sorry I did this to you. I have always wanted you for myself, but you wouldn't give me the time of day. You were so in love with Brian Kellogg and he told me if I ever laid eyes on you, he would kill me. I was so glad you asked me to take you home tonight, but I got fighting mad when you told me no, after I popped the question. Truly, I never meant to hurt you and now I cannot live with having hurt you so badly. By the time you read this letter, I will have blown my brains out. Stay sweet.

I love you Shaymin!

John Hensen

"Bring it on!" Shaymin screamed. "Give me some more. I'll never amount to anything; all my dreams have been shattered and now the man I thought I would spend the rest of my life with told me he cheated on me and has a two-year-old little girl. Nobody really wants me; all they ever want is my cookie box, and when they get that, they are gone quicker than they came."

Now greatly inebriated, she brought the bottle of White Zinfandel to her mouth and gulped down the rest. She threw the bottle on the floor and fell back onto the bed. She cried until she cried herself to sleep…

"Mm, mm, mm," Shaymin said as she began to dream. "Oh Roger, give it to me! Oh Roger, love me. Oh Roger, I need you. Oh Roger, you are so good. Oh Roger, hold me, hold me, and hold me…

"Oh no," Shaymin said as she awoke, "it is only a dream." She began to bang her head on the headboard, but quickly stopped when she realized she had a headache and a half. "Oh, my head hurts," she said. "No! No! No! Not another hangover! And a damn dream I wish could be reality…"

The phone rang. Shaymin groggily answered it. "Hello," she said.

"What in the world is wrong with you?" Roché asked.

"Well, I have a book I can read, write, or sell to you about what's wrong with me. Which way do you want it?" Shaymin asked as she massaged her temples. "Where do you want me to start?"

"Start from the beginning," Roché responded.

"Naw, I will give you the good news first. It is not much, nor is it realistic. I had a dream. Needless to say, I was blasted first. I fell asleep and dreamt that I was engaged in a compromising position with Roger."

"Oh girl, was this really a dream? On the other hand, are you trying to have me read between the lines? Or are you sending subliminal messages?" Roché asked.

"No Roché, really this was a dream. It was so good; I wish it were the real thing. Then I had to wake up, and I found myself alone and hung over as usual."

"Humph," Roché grunted, "well I am sorry you had a dream

L. Charmane Pough Chestnut

of that nature and weren't able to reenact it live."

"Girl, how do you think I feel?" Shaymin chimed in. "At least you have Josh to rock your world. Unfortunately I have no one but me, myself, and I."

"Stop tripping Shay," Roché said. "Joshua is a completely different entity. But what is up with Carlos?"

"Carlos? Who is Carlos?" Shaymin laughed aloud and then said, "Ouch, I forgot my damn head hurts. Carlos is history, finished, done, gone out of my life forever. Thank you Jesus, hallelujah, as Ashley would say. Speaking of which, we need to get together and get caught up on some things. I have something to tell y'all. My life has been a soap opera in the last three days. So much has transpired; I really could write a book. If anything else happens, I think I would just crack up and check myself into the crazy house. Oh by the way, I dreamt about fish the other night. Which one of you is pregnant? Is it you, Roché, or is it Ashley?"

"Hell to the no, for me," Roché quickly interrupted. "Who is to say it is not you, Shaymin? You know you love to get your groove on."

"No way," Shaymin quickly defended herself. "I am celibate, abstinent, goody two-shoes. Shaymin has not been involved for months. Surprised aren't you?"

"What's wrong with you?" asked Roché. "Have you turned in your player card, or have you been saved? Of course Ashley would shout for joy about that."

"Saved! No, not yet," Shaymin replied. "I have been thinking about it because of the way my life has been going lately. I need to try Jesus; I have basically tried everything else."

"Well then why don't you go to church with Harry and Ashley, or set up an appointment with Pastor and First Lady

Shelton. I am sure you see First Lady Shelton on a regular basis. She gets her hair done every week and she frequently shops in the dress boutique you have there in the salon. I am sure she is ready to minister to you, if you allow her to," Roché stated.

"You know Roché, I think it is time I consider a change in lifestyle. However, I am not sure I am ready to make such a drastic change and commitment," Shaymin said somberly. "I want to be all I can be and be serious about it; I don't want to get into it and then backslide. I do not want to be like so many Christians. You really can't tell the Christians from the sinners, or the saints from the ain'ts; everybody looks alike, dresses alike, talks and acts alike. So who is real and who is not? Hey, how about the three of us get together on Saturday and talk about what has been going on in our lives, our heads, and our fantasy worlds."

"That sounds great," Roché answered excitedly. "I will call Ashley and we will decide where to meet and we will see you there on Saturday. I will call you back and let you know where and when on Saturday, okay?"

"Okay, talk with you later." Shaymin added, "And Roché— I love you."

"I love you too, Shaymin," Roché said. "Bye-bye."

L. Charmane Pough Chestnut

Chapter Eighteen

SHAYMIN rolled over in bed and said to herself, I guess I will get some rest now. I do have a job to go to tomorrow. I just hope my head is not thumping and throbbing in the morning. My first client is uppity Mrs. Karsha Mankins; I don't feel like dealing with her mess in the morning. I remember the last time I did her hair, she waited until she got in the car, then turned around and came back into the salon to tell me she didn't like her hairstyle. Of course, I wanted to tell her where to get off, but I was very nice and pasted on a very phony smile and began to speak through my teeth. "Yes Mrs. Rankin, I will give you a free 'do the next time you come in." I wanted to splash a glass of hot water in her face, kick her in her butt, and dare her to come back to my salon again. It would have been a perfect time for a glass of hot water, since it was already a whooping ninety-five degrees outside. I can see all of her beautiful curly weave just hanging limp and frizzy. With that image in her mind, Shaymin laughed so hard she really became tickled and her head began to pound.

Shaymin lay back in her bed and flicked on the television. Whom did she hear but Bishop David J. Banks?

"If you can see it, you can have it. What are you waiting for?" Bishop Banks asked. "You have tried everything else; isn't it time you try Jesus? Jesus is the solution to every problem you have ever encountered. He will turn your mess into a message, your problems into praise, your situation into a sanctuary, and your tragedy into triumph. God wants you to know there is a treasure in those dark places. He wants to give you beauty for your ashes.

"He is waiting on you to allow him to turn your life around so that you can serve him with your whole heart, mind, body, and soul. I know you are wondering why your life is going the way that it is. It is because you have not made Jesus the center of your life. Jesus awaits you; Jesus awaits you; yes, Jesus awaits you. He wants you to know that you are better than your problems and greater than your circumstances. Your best days and your blessed days are ahead of you. You are more than a conqueror, and the devil cannot stop God from blessing you.

"I say to you, my sister, my brother, if you can see it, you can have it. Give God a chance to make it happen in your life. Become whole today; there is a void in your life and only Jesus can fill that void. Will you allow him to?"

Shaymin lay in her bed with tears streaming down her face and she said to God, "I know Bishop Banks is talking to me. My life is so screwed up and I know I need you. But God, I am not ready. I am not ready," she repeated as she began to cry uncontrollably... Eventually she drifted off to sleep again.

"I... I... I..." Shaymin screamed as she jumped up from her sleep. She remembered hearing "Come to Jesus; come to

Jesus." She remembered seeing herself falling off a cliff into what seemed to be a bottomless pit, which was well lit with flames of fire.

As Shaymin gathered herself from her nightmare, she grabbed a pen and some paper and began to write. While she wrote, she remembered that writing was once one of her favorite pastimes. She had gotten away from it because all she ever wrote about was the craziness going on in her life. There was always chaos and turmoil. To her, her life had been a category 10 hurricane, or an earthquake registered at 9.0 on a Richter scale.

Shaymin wrote:

Thursday September 6, 2:00 a.m.

Dear God,

I don't even think I have the right to write you a letter, but I am tired of myself and I need some help. I don't know what to do or where to start. I have considered being saved and starting to do the right things, but God, will that change anything? I look at Harry and Ashley, who are some of your key officials in the church, and they are so miserable. Please tell me, what can be added to my life by becoming saved?

Chadda, who works in the salon, says she is saved. Unfortunately, she has more problems than a zebra has stripes. According to what she says, nobody can ever do anything right except herself. But everybody always over-looks her and calls on her husband, Jaden, who is so calm and helpful. She could really be a great minister if she could get over herself and be considerate of others. Furthermore, who wants to be around a person who is so self-centered they can't see past themselves? Chadda tends to forget that she isn't the only person who breathes God's air. If nothing more, girlfriend can whip up some hair in no time—she does own the mold in doing hairstyles—that cannot be compared with or competed against.

Now God, back to my original question, why do I need to go to church? Wouldn't that be living a lie? I really don't think being saved is what I want or need. How can it be so right when I see so much wrong in many Christians? I can recite John 3:16 almost verbatim, "For God so loved the world, that he gave his only begotten son, that whosoever believeth in him should not perish, but have life everlasting." Please tell me God, why do I feel as if I am perishing right here on earth? And why do I believe in you? Why God, why? Can you please send me some help? Please give me some answers. Please...

After writing Shaymin began to doze again, but the ringing of the phone alarmed her. She quickly answered, "Hello!"

"Shaymin," Rockale said hysterically, "it is Alfonzo. He has been involved in a terrible accident. He flipped his truck five times and he was found unconscious. I just received the phone call; they are transporting him to Payne Harbor Medical Center as we speak."

"Okay," Shaymin said, "I will come and pick you up so you don't have to drive yourself to the hospital. I will be there shortly." She hung up the phone.

"Oh God," Shaymin murmured, "Here we go again—more tragedy and turmoil. My favorite cousin is now fighting for his life. There's nothing but turmoil after turmoil. How much more can I take? Oh, I need you Lord, more than I ever needed you before. And God, I am sorry. I know it seems like I am always complaining."

Oh! She thought. Whom can I call? We need someone to pray. Oh yeah, Pastor Shelton. But no, I am not a member of his church and it is 3:00 a.m. I can't call him this time in the morning. Ashley, Chadda, Chadda, Ashley.

"Oh Lord I need you," she blurted out, her voice trembling. She began to cry uncontrollably. "Please don't let Alfonzo die. Please, I know he isn't the best person in the world, but he is a good man. Yes, he has plenty of women, but overall he still has a great heart. I know he was probably drunk, but please spare my cousin."

She jumped into the car and fumbled with the radio station. As she was trying to find a gospel station, the radio began blasting The Dells. "Oh what a night?" she blurted out. "You got that right. Oh what a night?" As she tried to calm down, she shouted out, "Shoot! I do not know of any gospel stations and my life is nothing but a whirlwind. I will call Ashley when I get to the hospital and ask her to pray and ask her to call Pastor Shelton. I hope that he will pray for us because I am a friend of his faithful members, Harry and Ashley. And he knows I keep First Lady Shelton's hair smoking, so I am sure he will remember me and my family in his prayers."

Chapter Nineteen

SHAYMIN and Rockale finally reached the hospital safely. A police officer met them at the information desk; it was her duty to stay with the patient until a family member arrived. As Shaymin and Rockale approached the desk, the officer said that it was a miracle, Alfonzo made it through alive. She also stated that she did not issue him a DUI ticket, in the hope that this would give him a wake up call and he would stop drinking.

As Shaymin and Rockale settled in the waiting area, Shaymin picked up the phone and dialed Ashley's number. Ashley answered on the first ring. Shaymin said, "Ashley, hey girl, I know it is early in morning and I'm sorry to have to wake you up so early in the morning with my mess, but girl, I know you are a praying sister, and I need you to pray and to call Pastor Shelton and ask him to pray."

"Shaymin," Ashley interrupted, "what is the problem? Do you need me to come and get you or be with you?"

"No, I'm okay, but Alfonzo was in a terrible accident last

night. He flipped his car five times; he is in the intensive care unit with a slight concussion. They have him there to monitor him through the night. He is stable, but they still want to keep a close watch over him for the next twenty-four hours."

"How is Rockale?" Ashley asked. "Is she there with you? Do you need me to come to the hospital?"

"It is up to you girl," Shaymin responded. "I think I am about to lose my mind. Surprisingly, Rockale is holding up really well; it is me who is falling apart."

"All right Shaymin," Ashley stated, "do the best you can to keep your cool. I will call Roché and we will be there as soon as we can."

"Okay, thanks," Shaymin said as she hung up the phone.

"Rockale, how are you doing?" Shaymin asked.

"Oh girl, I am fine," Rockale responded. "I have learned how to call on the name of Jesus in many situations and He is my peace. I am learning how to trust God at all times—the good and the bad. There is no better time than now to cast my cares onto Him, for He cares for me. I have been praying for Alfonzo to get his life together. Maybe this will scare him enough and cause him to stop drinking and then driving. It probably would have been me, he was arguing with instead of Jackson, if I would argue with him. Fortunately, I have learned to release him to Jesus.

"He and Jackson were sitting in the basement doing their usual, drinking and shooting the jive. The conversation got rather heated, and you know your cousin Alfonzo—his temper is on a very short fuse, especially while drinking. The

L. Charmane Pough Chestnut

next thing I heard, they were loud and obnoxious and they began to push and scuffle. I tried to calm them down, but Alfonzo jumped in the car and sped out of the neighborhood like a bat out of hell. I immediately called 911 and explained to them what had just transpired, then gave a description of him and the car and the license plate number. About fifteen minutes later, I received a call from the police department. I praise God that it was not the other way. He should have been dead, but God spared his life. You heard the officer say she did not even give him a DUI ticket, and that hopefully this will scare him enough to stop drinking."

Shaymin was astonished. She looked at Rockale and said, "Well! Golly Gee! Are you save? And if so, when did this happen?"

"Yes, girl, I was saved August 3 at Forever Joy Outreach Ministries, where Curtis and Cathy Shelton are the Pastors," Rockale excitedly answered.

"Ashley's church?" Shaymin asked with a bewildered look.

"Yes, Ashley's and my church," Rockale said, still with the same excitement.

"Well I'll be damned—oh excuse me," Shaymin said, covering her mouth and holding her head down. "You know I have thought about it, but I do not think I am ready yet," she explained.

"Yessss, I have found a new joy and a new life, and life more abundantly in Jesus," Rockale exhaled.

"Well," Shaymin said abruptly, "I have found someone new also." Her mind quickly flashed on Roger. "But he is not Jesus. He may not even do me like Jesus, but to think of him do me is so, so, sooo good."

They both looked at each other and burst into laughter.

"Girl, you are crazy," Rockale stated. "No matter what the situation you can always make me laugh. Shaymin," Rockale spoke thoughtfully, "I will pray that you will one day make Jesus your choice. You will not regret it."

"Good morning ladies." The voice came from behind Shaymin and Rockale.

"Good morning Pastor and First Lady Shelton. What's up? Ashley and Roché?" Shaymin said.

"Good morning Pastor and First Lady Shelton. Hello Ashley, and Roché. Praise God and I thank you for coming so quickly," Rockale said.

"Oh it is our duty and a pleasure to come and see about our children. And you being one of our recent births, we had to come as soon as possible," First Lady Shelton responded, smiling beautifully.

"First Lady, your smile always brightens a gloomy day," Shaymin added.

"Thank you," First Lady said as she continued smiling.

"Well Sis Carpenter, how is Mr. Carpenter?" Pastor Shelton asked.

"Pastor, he is stable. They have him in the intensive care unit for the next few hours for observation. He suffered a slight concussion and they want to continue to monitor him closely. However, by the grace of God and all of your prayers, he will pull through this. Hopefully this will cause him to become a strong instrument of God and become a member of Forever Joy Outreach Ministries."

"Can we go in to see him now?" Pastor Shelton asked.

"Yes sir, Pastor, it is about that time. We can see him for ten minutes every hour," Rockale answered.

As they entered the room, Shaymin began to cry; Ashley immediately hugged her and tried to console her. Pastor Shelton grabbed one of Alfonzo's hands and First Lady Cathy grabbed his other hand. They then extended their hands to Rockale and the others.

"Father God in the name of Jesus," Pastor Shelton began to pray, "we thank you Lord, for this is the day that you have made and we shall rejoice and be glad in it. We lift Brother Carpenter up to you in the name of Jesus. Although the circumstances may look a little bleak to us, they are just right for you to work a miracle. For it is in our weaknesses that you are made strong. We trust Your Word that says that it is by your stripes we were healed in the name of Jesus. We know that you are the author and finisher of our faith. You have plans for our lives that are not evil, but give us an expected end. We trust you for a great outcome. In our worst situations, you have purpose and destiny; you see the end from the beginning, and everything we embark upon is a piece of the puzzle for our life's journey.

"We must go through and pass the test in order to have a testimony. We pray that this will be a testimony that will be shared throughout his life. We know that there are no accidents, but that you predestine everything, so that you can get the glory out of our lives. We thank you for a chance to be used by you, even in a tragic situation. We know you can turn this misery into a ministry. We thank you for blessing and consoling Sister Carpenter and the family, Shaymin, Ashley, and Roché. In addition, God, guide and instruct the doctors in the right way. Let your will be done in the name of Jesus, I pray. Amen."

Chapter Twenty

SHAYMIN sashayed into Right Way Café, and as always, she walked in with flirtatious and seductive gestures. "Hey, hey, hey," she said as she approached Ashley and Roché's table.

"Hey," they respond in unison.

"Sit your hot tail down," Roché quickly said to Shaymin.

"'Hot,' no, I have slowed my role. I am almost a saint like Ashley," They all laughed.

"You are crazy," Ashley responded.

"How's Alfonzo?" Roché asked.

"Oh, he is blessed and highly favored. Isn't that how y'all saved folks talk, Ashley? Ha, ha," Shaymin laughed. "No but seriously," Shaymin expounded, "Alfonzo is really a miracle and he is doing great. He is conscious, out of the intensive care unit, and talking a whole lot of noise again, so thank God he is back to normal. He does have to undergo surgery tomorrow on a fractured jawbone, and he does have a lot of recuperation to do, but overall he is doing wonderfully. The medical staff said that his recovery was a miracle that God performed right before their eyes. Hallelujah, thank you Jesus," Shaymin said jokingly.

"I know you are all about jokes, and that is okay, but all praises do go to Jesus who has spared Alfonzo's life," Ashley responded.

"Hallelujah," Shaymin said again as she jerked and threw her hands in the air. "Y'all know me by now. I love to have fun, so do not take me seriously Ashley, with your holy self."

"Well now girls, what has been going on in your lives?" Shaymin asked.

"Let me speak first," Roché said quickly. "My news is more exciting than any of yours."

"Says who?" Ashley asked.

"Says me," responded Roché. "I have been bad, or maybe I should say I've been a good girl in Shane's world."

"Shane! Who the hell is Shane?" Shaymin questioned.

"Be quiet and let me finish please," Roché chimed in again. "Shane is my high school friend who is truly my soul mate. I recently called his parents, got his number, called him, and the rest is history."

"Okay, we have time to hear about your history-making ordeal, so continue to talk," Shaymin said as she bobbed her head from side to side.

Roché began to reminisce, "Now getting his number was the first hurdle, but I faced another hurdle as I looked at Shane's phone number, contemplating whether or not to dial the number. My voice of reason convinced me that I had waited so long, that it was time for me to be true to myself and at least clear my mind by expressing my true feelings. I immediately dialed the number before I had time for second thoughts.

"A strong, sexy voice answered, 'Hello, this is Shane Jefferson.'"

"I hesitated then said, 'Hey Shane! It's me Roché.'"

"Shane quickly replied, 'Hey girl, what a pleasant surprise. How are you?'"

"'I am great,' I responded. 'I was thinking of you and I know it has been a long time since we have been in contact. I called your parents and got your number. I hope that's okay. I have been thinking about old times and the awesome friendship that we had.'"

"Shane said, 'Okay, so what are you trying to say?'

"'All right, all right. I love you and always have since that incredible kiss we shared before you left for college. I have had an insatiable longing for you all of these years and just now got the nerve to verbalize it to you. I understand you may not feel the same way but I need to be true to myself and let you know my real feelings for you.'"

"Shane surprisingly responded, 'I am just blown away. I have felt the same way since the first time I laid eyes on you. I would have never guessed you had those kinds of feelings for me. I am so relieved. So where do we go from here?'

"I said, 'I will not be able to see you and not touch you, so let's just stay in touch for now and maybe later we can schedule a meeting place.'

Then I thought, "'No, hell no. I need to see you now, now that we have laid everything on the table. I have held back my feelings for way too long; please do not deny me this life-altering opportunity.'

"So we scheduled a meeting for the following week during the day while our spouses and children were at work and school. We ended our conversation by exchanging contact information and reiterating our affection for each other.

"And that's all the history y'all need to know about me and Shane," Roché finished, still in a daze as she remembered their meeting.

"Ah hell no," Shaymin said. "You are going to give the scoop on the day y'all met, because you still have a glow, so I know he rocked your world inside out. So come on with the come on. You ain't nothing but a big ole heifer. Tell us the rest of the story," Shaymin laughed hilariously.

"Okay, but be quiet so that I can talk about our rendezvous," Roché began to speak. "Shane arrived at the Madison Bed and Bath to prepare and make sure I would be lavished with all the romance he had longed to administer to me for so long now. He said his wish, his dream, and his desire had finally become a reality. He had candles lit throughout the entire room and rose petals lined a path from the door to the breakfast nook. There he sat, looking drop-dead gorgeous. He sang, 'Don't you remember you told me you loved me baby, you said you would be coming back this way again; if only for one night.' I was so nervous, I was sweating bullets and I didn't know what to do with myself."

"So what happened next?" Shaymin interjected.

"Be quiet girl, let me finish. I got to take it slow, because I am reliving this thing and I don't want it to ever end," Roché whispered, her eyes filled with tears. She continued, "Shane

L. Charmane Pough Chestnut

stood up, kissed me passionately, and then began to remove my red sleeveless dress, which was accented with matching red lingerie, and uh, uh, uh, uh, the rest is history… Shane, Shane, Shane…"

"Slap that heifer, Ashley. Wake her up out of her dream," Shaymin blurted out.

"Oh yeah, I was dreaming a good dream," Roché whispered. "He rocked my world."

"So what are you going to tell Josh?" asked Ashley.

"Tell Joshua!" Roché exclaimed. "Probably hello, and good-bye. My road is open for only Shane to drive on, and it is a one-way lane that leads to a place where only Shane can park, and he can stay as long as he likes." She burst into laughter.

"So then you are probably the one who is pregnant. I told you I dreamt about fish the other night," Shaymin smiled.

"Yeah and I told you, 'Hell to the no' the other day too!" Roché rolled her eyes and bobbed her head. "I am not preg-nant. It could very well be Ashley, because Harry's still got it going on," she joked, "at least that is the rumor at the salon, oops did I say that."

"Mm, mm, mm," Ashley moaned as she began to tell her story. "Lately I have been reminiscing about a grand event, escapade, and rendezvous I experienced about five years ago. I never intended to tell either of you, but I thought about it and realized I need to fess up before I mess up. After I reveal to y'all what happened, just call Pastor and First Lady Shelton and have them take me straight to the altar of repen-tance and pray my strength in the Lord.

"Y'all I was at a Psychology Association Convention in Waikiki, Hawaii. The minute I stepped off the plane, I felt a wave of excitement come over me. I really did not know what was going on until I stepped into the Biltmore Hotel and Suites. I saw him standing at the bar alone. I was thirsty from my ride from the airport and decided to go to the bar for a drink. Oh, what an everlasting drink I got; the lady at the well ain't got nothing on me. She thought Jesus gave her a drink, but Keagan gave me a drink I will never forget.

"As I approached the bar, I locked eyes with Keagan Hodges. We were there in Hawaii for one week, and he truly made one weak—me. He made me weak and then he strengthened me again all in the same exercise, Instead of 'Oh what a night,' it was 'Oh what a week.' He made me feel like the lady I always needed to feel like, always yearned to feel like."

"Hold up, wait a minute," Shaymin interrupted with her hands in the air as if she was under arrest, "you mean to tell me, and you met this Keagan— and Keagan, that name sounds white; is he white Ashley? Girl, tell me how is it with a white man? I always wanted to try one. Girlfriend, looking at you, I know I have to find me one now, because he seems to have rocked your world… But as I was saying, you met this Keagan in the Biltmore and slept with him all week long?"

"Yep," Ashley answered, "and I am not ashamed, nor do I regret any moment of it."

"You whore, whore, whore," Shaymin laughed. "Roché you hear that? Miss Holy Ashley met Keagan for the first time at the Biltmore Hotel and became his mistress for the week."

"You must understand," Ashley butted in, "this happened shortly after I was saved. I was not as rooted and grounded in the Word as I am now, and furthermore, Harry and I were separated at the time. However, Keagan Hodges turned my world inside out and upside down, in every way and position

L. Charmane Pough Chestnut

he could. He made it sooo right. Every night was a night to remember, but our last night was the most memorable. Keagan and I spent the last night in a beautiful resort owned by one of his friends. He planned every moment, from the wild cherries to the whipped cream. He also managed to get lilies in every color, knowing they were my favorite flowers. He touched every essence of my being until every fiber of my skin was screaming, 'Encore!'"

"Roché, slap that girl back into reality," Shaymin said. "She has to go home to Harry and she cannot go and call Keagan's name in Harry's house."

They all laughed in unison.

Chapter Twenty-One

SHAYMIN threw her hands in the air in disbelief and yelled, "Call the law! The two of you need to be arrested for infidelity. Here I am trying to get my life together, considering being saved, and planning my marriage, and now the two of you have just dropped a bomb on me. Fortunately, you have helped me decide not to marry Carlos. Now that I have heard about the rendezvous you two have experienced, I know it is the right decision." She snapped her fingers and clapped her hands. "Yep, the decision has been made."

"Shaymin, did you say you were considering being saved?" asked Ashley. "Hallelujah, thank you Jesus, and glory to the good Lord and the sanctified beat."

"What! You are not going to marry Carlos?" Roché asked in surprise.

"Yeah why not?" Ashley asked.

Shaymin began to tell her story. "It all started at Alfonzo's party. Roger and I were lounging by the pool and then in walked Carlos, who was supposed to be out of town on a business trip. It was not a pretty picture. I tried to explain to him that Roger and I were only friends, but Carlos did not believe me. He stormed out of the door and flew out of the neighborhood. He came over the next day. We made up and tried to discuss our wedding plans until he dropped the bomb about little Miss Shaymin Monaé."

"Shaymin Monaé! Who the hell—I mean who she is?" Ashley inquired, ashamed at her language. "Sorry, the old Ashley sprung up for a moment."

"Shaymin Monaé is Carlos' two-year-old daughter. He manages to go and see her every holiday on his, quote unquote, business trips," Shaymin said sarcastically.

"Oh my God," said Roché.

"Oh no," said Ashley.

"Yes, this is why Carlos is always out of town every holiday. He goes to see his daughter whom he named after me. He said he named her that because he wanted a part of me in his life always. He said he knew if I ever found out about his daughter, that he would be history."

"That two-timing, good-for-nothing dog. I knew there was something going on. As the Bible says, what's done in the dark will surely come to the light. I am sorry," Ashley, said, "it just seems like the last few episodes have been bringing out the worst in me. Please forgive me, girls. So where does that leave you and Roger?"

"Actually, I really don't know," Shaymin responded nonchalantly. "I don't know what's going on with Roger. Don't get me wrong, I really like Roger, but I think he has a hidden agenda. I am getting mixed signals and uneasy vibes from him. I think he may be married. He has never said anything about a wife, but my woman's sixth sense tells me that there is something, he is hiding. I have never received a call from him at home and I only have his work number. I have been to his house on one occasion; the day after I met him he took me there so he could change his clothes, but we have never gone to his home again. I do know where he lives. Maybe I will do a drive by one day. I think there's something fishy there, what do y'all think?"

"Now remember, you are engaged," added Ashley.

"You mean I was engaged," Shaymin responded quickly.

"Was, is, or whatever it is," Ashley said, "Have you thought that maybe Roger doesn't want to get hurt? The main thing he knows about you is that you are, or were, supposed to be engaged, and sometimes the less you know about people the better off you will be."

"Yeah, yeah, whatever," Shaymin smirked, "I thought being married was one of the greatest journeys I would ever embark upon. I thought it would be one of the most exciting and fulfilling episodes in my life. Every mother is always excited about her beautiful daughter finding the man of her dreams, becoming his bride, and bringing forth grandbabies for Grandma to spoil rotten. Now I am seeing another side of marriage. And my mother could care less as to whether I find a good man or have a baby because she never wanted me anyway."

"Now Shaymin, don't go bashing your mother or marriages," Ashley said. "Thank God that someone did take you in and show you some love and attention. Always look on the positive side. Your mother could have had an abortion. Also you could have been left in an orphanage. Just be glad that someone did adopt you, so that in itself is a blessing.

"Also, marriage is honorable and the bed is undefiled, but

when you have two imperfect people coming together under one roof, there will always be some misunderstandings, some hurt feelings, and some days of trouble. I will say," Ashley, continued, "make sure you know who you are marrying. Make sure the two of you have the same goals and dreams in mind and that the two of you agree to work together in order to achieve your goals. You need to become best friends first, and then let that grow into a love affair. Don't just jump for him because he is fine, because that fine may become fat and that smile may become toothless and then you will be back to square one again, unhappy.

"So make sure he is your soul mate and both of you are willing to give 100 percent. Then life and love will be a splendid thing. Don't let anyone cloud your mind by telling you that marriage is fifty-fifty. Marriage will always work when the two of you are willing to give 100 percent. Having God, as the center of your marriage is the main objective; it will give you a great line of communication. However, without communication, you will have a dead marriage.

"When bound together with your soul mate, it will never be a problem giving, sharing, and doing for each other. In fact, the two of you might find yourselves competing to please each other by cooking, cleaning, lavishing each other with gifts, and romancing each other. There will never be a dull moment in your house.

"The worst thing you could do is become a nagging wife, for it is better to be on the rooftop of a house than in the house with a nagging wife—or a trifling husband for that matter. A trifling husband is worse than an infidel." Ashley shook her head as she spoke.

"When you do get married," she said, "always do your best to keep your spouse happy. And remember if you don't keep your spouse happy, there is always someone out there who will do a better job than you are willing to do. You may be saying, 'Shoo, fly, shoo,' while there is someone on the other side of the street saying, 'Here kitty, kitty.' Don't ever say the grass is greener on the other side of the fence, because if you choose the right grass, then water and fertilize it properly, it will grow and satisfy your every need. Now let the church say Amen…

"Shaymin," Ashley continued, "I said all of that just to say that if you do not think Carlos is your soul mate and you are having second thoughts about marrying him, then I think you might need to wait on God and have Him connect the right man to you. Wait on God; He has the perfect plan for your life. I wish I had waited."

"Amen to that!" shouted Roché.

Shaymin responded, "I thank you girls for being my best friends and for coaching me on the marriage thing. I think I wanted to get married for all the wrong reasons: my age, wanting to have babies in wedlock, and being sick of people always asking me if I had gotten married yet. Once again, thank you for enlightening me on the pros and cons of marriage, because I really want to marry my soul mate. I want marital bliss, not marital misery. I do not want to end up like you two ole biddies who are miserable in your choice of a husband, but pretty much stuck because of the kids.

"Speaking of kids, one of you is pregnant. I dreamt about fish the other night. You may not fess up now, but soon, very soon, one of you will make that announcement. Ha, ha, already stuck in your marriage and now about to have another baby. Now isn't that a blimp," Shaymin laughed.

Chapter Twenty-Two

SHAYMIN threw her hands in the air and waved to her girls. "Well girls, it has been a pleasure as always to hang with the two of you. I am going to plant you now and dig you later," Shaymin stated as she slid into her car. "Yo Ashley, I might see you in church tomorrow. I feel an urge to be in the service one more time." She laughed and started her car's engine.

Ashley said, "It would be a joy to have you in service with us tomorrow. I am sure Pastor Shelton will have a word hot off the press with your name on it, just waiting for you to believe, perceive, and receive it. Yes, come on girl, you will have a great time. Who knows, tomorrow may be your day of salvation. How about you Roché, when are you going to join us in praising the Lord?"

"How does Alfonzo say it...? When they get a bar and a smoking section." The three of them burst into laughter.

"Oh yeah," Shaymin said, "Before I forget, Mercedes is having a Halloween party on October 31. Would you ladies like to come with me?"

"Well Shaymin," Ashley nodded her head, "I really don't do Halloween. We do Hallelujah night at church, but I may go just to see some of the silly costumes worn that night."

"As for me," Roché exclaimed, "I might go. But I may need to do some tricks or get a treat, because the old bag I have at home seems to have forgotten how to treat me with love and romance. But who knows, I might be right there in my Wonder Woman costume."

"Very good Roché, please come. It is going to be at Club 2000 on Ashton Boulevard. I have yet to decide who I am gonna be. I might be Jeannie from 'I Dream of Jeannie.' Maybe I can use some of my magic and trick Roger into the bed, car, or woods. I am sure any of those places would be a great place for Roger and me," Shaymin smiled flirtatiously and batted her eyes. "I wonder what's up with him. I haven't heard from him for a few days now. Ooh, I tell you that is one fine hunk of chocolate-covered pecans, and you two know how I love my chocolate-covered nuts."

"Speaking of Roger isn't that Roger and a pregnant lady and a little boy entering Jack B Quick restaurant?" asked Ashley. "I wonder who that lady and the little boy could be. She must be a client or his sister or something of that nature. He is not married is he?"

"Well I don't know," Shaymin responded, "he has never talked about a wife or a family, so I really don't know who that is with him." Shaymin smiled and waved at her girls as she slowly drove off. She turned her head slightly toward Jack B Quick to get a second look and to be certain that it was Roger and his precious little family.

Shaymin didn't quite know why, but she felt betrayed. She thought of the woman and the little boy. Could it be? She asked herself. Could it be his pregnant wife and his little boy? I guess that explains why I only have his work number, he calls me so seldom, and for the most part whenever I call him, he is busy. He has a wife and a family. No, no, no. I knew it was too good to be true. I knew there was more than what was on the surface. As the old folks always say, "Keep on living; the truth will eventually be revealed." However, I like him, I want him, but he has so many strings attached. He has a wife, a baby on the way, and a son; there is no way I can be the fourth leg. No, no, there is no way. I may as well go on and get saved or maybe even become a nun. However, if I become a nun then I should have no desire for men; I will only love the Lord and His desires for my life. But if I get saved these hormones of mine won't be saved and I will still want a man, every now and again, so why don't I stop fooling myself. Yes, I think I will go and talk to a priest about becoming a nun, or at least find what the criterion of becoming one is.

As Shaymin began to cry, the radio played, "If you can't be with the one you love, love the one you are with."

"Hell, how can you love the one you are with, if you don't have anyone to be with?" Shaymin screamed. "There is Carlos who cheated on me and has a little girl, there were my two boyfriends prior to Carlos who cheated on me, and now it turns out Roger has a wife and a family." Well, Shaymin thought, I probably can't depend on them to be Dr. Feelgood, but I can always call on my best friends Hennessey and White Zinfandel. They always make my liver quiver and give me a good sensual shiver from my head to my toes. Yes, that is exactly what I will do; I will get me two men, White and Zinfandel, and take them home with me. They won't leave until I am finished with them. That sounds like a great idea. In fact, there is a liquor store right there... But where the hell am I? She wondered as she wiped the tears from her eyes. Oh man, I have driven ten miles past my house.

Shaymin pulled up to the liquor store, jumped out of the car, and ran in. "Hi Raymond," she said as she read his nametag. "I want to purchase two of your men to go home with me tonight."

"Ma'am, I am sorry I must have misunderstood you," Raymond said as he scratched his head and stretched his eyes while he stared at Shaymin. "We don't sell men here, however, down the street there is a strip joint where you may be able to find one or two."

"Now that's not a bad idea," Shaymin replied. "A one-night stand may be better than trying to have a long-term relationship, but naw… I want them two right there in the bottle, White and Zinfandel. I know they won't leave until I'm finished with them; no they won't leave me for another woman." As she paid Raymond, she asked for a cup, then laughed aloud and ran out of the store.

"Hello," Roché answered the phone.

"Hey girl," Ashley responded, "have you heard from Shaymin? It's been about two hours. I have been calling her house, but there is no answer and her cell phone goes straight to her voicemail. Do you think our girl is okay? I know she was upset today when she saw Roger and the family out and about. She was just imagining how it would be to get with Roger and then that family scene pops right up in her face. I know she is hurt about the Carlos incident. I am concerned about her, because you know how she does; she has probably gone somewhere and gotten her drink on

L. Charmane Pough Chestnut

and fallen out. I pray for her safety. Give me a holler if you hear anything."

"Well Ashley, I agree, because you know how Shaymin is; she always gets her a temporary fix for all of her problems. As she would say, three of her favorite men are Hennessey, White, and Zinfandel. So she probably has chosen one or two of them and drank them and fallen out. If we don't hear from her tonight then we will go in the morning and check on her."

"Okay Roché, holler at me as soon as you hear from her," Ashley responded.

Chapter Twenty-Three

"LADY..." Shaymin heard a deep baritone voice coming from behind her. At least she thought it was coming from behind her. She jumped and looked around; clearly not realizing the man was right smack in front of her. "Lady," he continued, "you need to wake up and go home. Well, you don't have to go home, but you must leave here because we are closed."

"Closed! Where the hell am I?" Shaymin asked. "Oh, my head hurts. Who the hell are you?"

"You are at Club Utopia, where you probably spent your whole paycheck with all of the dollars you put in the strippers' G-strings last night. I will say you were having a good ole time and I am sure the strippers really appreciated you. They probably received more money from you last night than they received all week long. You were putting it out. If I weren't who I am, I probably would have put on a G-string so you could have given me some m-o-n-e-y. Fortunately, I am Johnson, Officer Sean Johnson, the security guard. Can

I escort you safely to your car?"

"Escort me to my car!" Shaymin's speech was very slurred. She had consumed both bottles of White and Zinfandel before entering Club Utopia. "Officer Johnson, that... that's..." she stuttered and paused, "what you say your name is right? Why don't you take me home and use your handcuffs and we can play cops and robbers? You will be the robber and I will be the cop. I will handcuff you to my bed and make you call 'Shaymin' all night long..." Shaymin said as she glided her hand across Officer Johnson's chest.

He gently grabbed her hand and said, "No ma'am, lady, Shaymin—that is your name right? I know my faith and my line of work, or at least where I am working tonight, do not seem to coincide with each other. Nevertheless, I am a happily married man of God with two beautiful daughters at home, so there is no way I could consent to what you are trying to initiate.

"Furthermore, the beautiful Nubian queen that you are, you should not be making advances at me or any other man. This type of behavior is too dangerous. Is there someone I can call to come and pick you up? I really don't think you should drive yourself home tonight; you have had too much to drink."

"Well Officer John... John... Johnson," Shaymin stuttered, "I do not have to drive; you can drive me home and to bed— or anywhere you would like to drive me to, as a matter of fact—ly." Shaymin laughed and her head began to bob up and down. It was clear she had had far too many drinks.

"No lady!" Officer Johnson said in stern voice. His mannerisms began to change; he was a little frustrated with Shaymin. "No Shaymin. That will not be happening. I have too much respect for you, my wife, and for myself to commit such a dishonorable act. Now, so that you are not hurt or killed tonight, whom may I call to get you home safely?"

"Ooh officer, your aggressiveness turns me on and I like your voice," she said very slowly. She threw her arms around the officer's neck and began to sob. "Why, why, why? All I want is a little love. All I need is for someone to hold me tight. I juuust," she slowly drew the word out, "found out my ex-fiancé has a two-year-old little girl. And to top that off, the man I thought was my soul mate, I just saw him to—tonight with his wife and family. Now you tell me no. All I want is to be loved. Why can't you love me? Why can't you hold me?"

"Shaymin," Officer Johnson said, "what you are requesting is not love; it is lust and infatuation and a temporary fix for the pain you are experiencing. To grant you your request would only add insult to injury, because you would wake up in the morning sober, regret ever seeing me, and be embarrassed over your behavior.

"I can't grant your request, but I can offer you Jesus Christ. He will love you unconditionally; He will give you everything you need, and He will comfort you and heal all your past hurts. He will be with you through the thick and the thin, through the good and the bad. He will not use your body or mind for his own personal gain. His plan for you is to give you hope and an expected end, not to harm you."

"I know, I know, I have heard about that Jesus man and all that he will, can, and wants to do. I have even thought about trying him; but every time I think about doing it, something awful always happens to me. I even had plans to go to church this morning, but look where I ended up, and it is only because I saw my Roger with his family. Roger had me thinking it would be him and me for the rest of our lives.

Huh, he did as they all do—he lied…

"Can I use your phone?" Shaymin asked somberly. "I will call Roché and she will come and get me. Will my car be okay here until I can come and get it later today?"

"Yes ma'am, it will. Here is the phone. Or do you need me to dial the number for you?" asked Officer Johnson.

"Will you please dial the number for me—573-8790," Shaymin blurted out the numbers.

"Here Shaymin, the phone is ringing," Officer Johnson said.

"Hello," Roché sounded startled.

"Hi Roché, it is me. Can you come and pick me up?"

"Shaymin, are you okay? And where are you?" Roché asked.

"Yes Roché, I am fine; just drunk as usual. After seeing Roger and company today, I couldn't handle it. I ended up buying my favorite, White and Zinfandel, and drove myself to Club Utopia on Harlem Street and the rest is history. Now Officer Johnson will not let me drive home drunk," Shaymin explained to Roché.

"Okay Shaymin, I will be there as soon as possible," Roché replied. "I don't know what I am going to do with you girl."

"You can't do nothing but love me; I am just like your child —you always have to bail me out of something. Thank you Roché, and thank you Officer Johnson." She hung the phone up and continued, "Thank you for being a real man and please forgive me for my awful behavior."

"Shaymin, I give God the glory for making me the man that I am. There was a time when I probably would have taken you up on your request, but I thank God that I am now a changed man. My job is to protect you, not to administer pain."

Chapter Twenty-Four

SHAYMIN said good morning to First Lady Shelton as Lady Shelton sashayed glamorously into the salon, looking like a beautiful diva. She always looked as fresh and crisp as new money.

"How is everybody doing?" Lady Shelton asked as she took a seat in Shaymin's chair.

"Lady Shelton," Chadda said from her styling station, "I want to look, dress, and smile just like you when I grow up. You are always so stunning every time I see you. And you have the audacity to come and get your hair done when there is not a strand of your hair out of place as it is. I am sure Shaymin doesn't mind because you sure do keep her in business—you have a standing appointment every week. Hot dog," Chadda said as she snapped her fingers, "you got it going on, and that's why I want to be just like you."

Shaymin thought, Chadda, with her ghetto self, actually managed to get that entire speech out in one breath. Yes, ghetto!

"Well ladies," Lady Shelton began to speak, "I guess I am going to have to come and give a class to you young ladies on how to be fifty and fabulous." She stood up and strode across the floor as if she were modeling for the entire salon. "Now how many of you will attend?" Everyone in the salon, including the clients, all said they would and laughed in unison.

"Lady Shelton, I believe that you are a lot of fun," Shaymin said. "I have the perfect outfit for you. I ordered it only in your size, because only you can wear this one with enough pizzazz. So on top of your free hairdo, I am going to give you the entire outfit. I just want to see you in that outfit. I know you will wear it with class. Please take a picture and give it to me."

"Sweetie, that is truly a blessing and I really appreciate you doing this. If you tell me when you are coming to church I will make sure to have it on then," Lady Shelton said.

"Now, now, Lady Shelton, I don't want to lie to you or God; I really don't know when I will be there. I will say I have had an urge and a desire to come to church, but I have not made up my mind yet. So in the meanwhile please pray for me," Shaymin suggested.

"Shaymin, line two," Audra announced over the intercom. "It is Roché."

"Hello this is Shaymin. What's up girl?" Shaymin asked.

"Shaymin, I just came from the doctor and guess what?" Roché said.

"Girl, I told you somebody was pregnant. Girl, when I dream about fish, you had better believe somebody is pregnant,"

Shaymin blabbered.

"Yes I am pregnant—eight weeks," Roché said somberly.

Shaymin laughed hilariously while trying not to lose her composure. "Roché are you serious?" she asked. "Remember I told you I dreamt about fish and my dreams aren't often wrong."

"Girl," Roché said softly, "the only thing I am concerned with is that I don't know if it is Joshua's or Shane's. In a way, I hope it is Shane's, because I am in love with Shane. However, on the other hand, it had better be Joshua's so that he doesn't kill me and the baby."

"Well girlfriend, I am doing Lady Shelton's hair now, so I will ask her to pray for you and your dilemma. I will call Ashley and ask her to pray also. Actually, I just asked Lady Shelton to pray for me concerning my change of lifestyle. I am sure she will not mind sending up a prayer for you too. I know they love interceding on behalf of us sinners." Shaymin whispered to Roché, "If you were living right, you would not be worried." She continued to laugh.

"Shaymin," Roché said, stop tripping, do me a favor, and tell Lady Shelton hello and thanks

"Will do girl."

"Goodbye," they said in unison.

"Is Roché okay?" Lady Shelton asked.

"Yes ma'am, she is just pregnant," Shaymin answered.

"Pregnant! Great! She is married with children, so one more will not hurt. Tell her congratulations," Lady Shelton said.

"Yes ma'am, I guess you are right," Shaymin said as she laughed to herself. She thought, Lady Shelton really does not understand the drama behind Roché being pregnant.

"Um, Lady Shelton please tell me why it seems as if some people are born with a silver spoon in their mouths and everything falls into place for them, from childhood to old age. Unfortunately, on the other hand, someone like me—nothing ever goes right for me. I can't get a clean break in life. I can't seem to keep a boyfriend; they always cheat on me. I have been raped, molested, and just downright abused by men. I do want a good, lasting relationship, but it never seems as if I can meet the right man. Does God have favorite children? Because it seems like I am one of the ones that he just despises. Therefore, I just get drunk and fall out. I try to drink my problems away. Then, as always, I wake up hung over and the problem has become like a disease and metastasized. I could tell you so much that has gone on in my life, but I don't want to bother you with my many mountains."

"Shaymin," Lady Shelton began to explain, "I tell you this from what I have heard thus far. Because of your mess, you are the perfect candidate for God to work a miracle in your life. In addition, no, God does not have favorite children; actually, He has no respect for persons. He reigns over the just as well as the unjust. Problems always come to make you strong. It is in difficult times when your weaknesses are made strong through God's strength. I will say this, in order to know that your problems are for your good, and for God's glory, you must develop a relationship with Him and begin to seek Him for your purpose and destiny in life. God will then carry you through your problems. It will be hard sometimes, but knowing that God is carrying you through gives you a sense of relief because it lets you know that you are not alone.

"You need to know that all things work together for the good of those who love the Lord and who are called according to His purpose. Therefore, sweetie, please consider getting saved and then we can help you get started on the right track and begin to walk according to the plans Jesus has for you. "Do you know that you are an original? When God made you, he broke the mold. There are no identical DNA's.

"Once you are saved, you will find out that your problems are your stepping stones and not obstacles or hindrances, in fact, they are your elevators. Consequently, through every obstacle that you encounter God is depositing something that you will be able to use later in life. If God allows it that means that, He has a purpose. In order to have a testimony you must go through a test. God allows you to go through so that you will be able to minister to someone who is going through the same test. I say let God use you. Your reward is far greater than what you are going through. The size of your problem is an indication of the size of your future."

"Thank you Lady Shelton,"Shaymin said as she sniffled and tried to hide her tears. "I know that you are in my corner and I appreciate you. I also know that God is in my corner, it just seems sometimes as if I am left out here all alone."

"I know baby," Lady Shelton concurred, "but remember, God will never leave you and never forsake you…"

Chapter Twenty-Five

"FREAK OUT! Le freak, c'est chic. Freak out! Le freak, c'est chic," Shaymin sang as she danced all alone and all over the floor to the beat of "Le Freak." She was feeling very good; she had had two glasses of Hennessey on the rocks and was starting to feel their effect.

"Kinda," Shaymin called out as she watched Ashley stride across the floor. "And is that Hondra Woman with you? It must be Roché. Kinda, you know when the clock strikes twelve you must be home or you will turn back into the old maid in the shoe. So what happened? Why aren't you at Hallelujah night? Or did you think Keagan would be here so you could get your freak on again?" Shaymin gave Ashley a bewildered look and winked her eye.

"Well Beanie, if you use your magic you can spare me a couple hours and I can stay a little while past twelve. Besides, Harry has given me a curfew and I must be home by twelve anyway."

"Damn Harry," Shaymin blurted out. "I am sorry Ashley,

you know I have had one too many drinks and I was just kidding. However, you are grown and you should be able to go home when you are ready. I know he comes home when he chooses to, if he chooses to come home at all. But I am sure he doesn't choose to come very often anyway, with all the commotion that goes on down there at the Mane and Tail Grooming Salon."

"Shhh…" Roché whispered to Shaymin, indicating that she be quiet.

"I am sorry," Shaymin said. "It is the Hennessey. And Hondra Woman, where is your Hondra Man?"

"Whom could you be referring to?" Roché asked. "Joshua is at home babysitting and Shane—ooh yes, Shane—he is probably with his wife tonight. So what about you Beannie, have you heard from Roooger?"

"Roger who?" Shaymin asked sarcastically. "Screw Roger. And the boat he came in on. I told you I am going to become a drunken nun. Ha, ha, ha. Picture that, a drunken nun. I am going to leave men alone and just drink myself silly."

"Now that's not good," said Roché.

"May not be, but this Hennessey sure has me feeling good right about now. Really, it feels better than sex—especially sex with the two-timers I have been involved with."

"Hey pretty lady, or should I say Beanie?" The voice came from behind Shaymin. "If I make a wish can

you make it come true by wiggling your nose or your toes, or can I make your toes wiggle for you?"

"It depends on whether or not you use the right tools, Teddy

Krueger. By the way, what is your name?"

"My name is Mason," the man said.

"Oh, hell no," Shaymin replied. "I might be drunk, but I have sense enough to know not to flirt with you. You are dressed like Teddy Krueger and named Mason. You are probably some serial killer. Your birthday is probably Friday the 13th. I don't trust you as far as I can see you; believe me I do have twenty-twenty vision. I can smell a snake from far off. You are probably just like any other guy I have dated, a wolf in sheep's clothing. Furthermore, I do not have time for a bunch of shucking and jiving. I have pretty much given up on men, because all of you are dogs—big dogs, little dogs, just a whole pack of dogs."

"So... um, what is your name?" Mason asked.

"Shaymin!"

"Therefore Shaymin, you are gay."

"And if I am, so what?" Shaymin replied. "But I am not gay; I've just been hurt by so many men and have decided to become a drunken nun."

"Shaymin," Mason said, "I do not know anything about religion, but I do know that drunk and nun do not go together."

"Well, call it something new Shaymin has invented and I will have it patented and copyrighted. Anyhow Mr. Mason Teddy Krueger, please leave me the hell alone, so I can get my groove on." Shaymin quickly spun onto the dance floor and began to sing and dance to "The Beat Goes On."

"Ouch," Shaymin squirmed as she tried to turn over in her hospital bed in Grover Palmetto Hospital.

Shaymin was bandaged from head to toe. She was rape and brutally beaten by Mason Teddy Krueger. The maniac had left her for dead after he had had his way with her at Mercedes' Halloween party.

"Roché," Ashley said as she shook her head, "as bad as this may sound, I believe that Shaymin probably led this crazy man on and then he turned on her, took what he wanted, beat her half to death, and left her for dead. You know Shaymin's whole demeanor is very flirtatious; she is not aware of how she flirts because it is so natural to her."

Roché shook her head and said, "Ashley you could be right, but no one deserves to be treated so badly. Besides, rape is never about sex anyway—it is always about violence. Therefore, whoever did this horrific thing must have been mad and wanted to hurt someone. It probably stemmed from his childhood. You know everything that you encounter in childhood usually follows you into adulthood and tends to cause numerous problems. If these things would be dealt with at an early age they would not haunt you in your future."

"Nevertheless," Ashley said, "whether Shaymin initiated it or not, she doesn't deserve this type of treatment. The maniac needs to be punished. In fact, I will make sure I get Roger on the case. I have his card and I will call as soon as possible."

"Call him?" Roché inquired. "Ashley, he is walking through the door as we speak." Roché called out to him, "Roger, it is so good to see you. I am so glad you came. I know Shaymin will be ecstatic to know you are here to see her. Did Joshua call you?" Oh Lord, Ashley, there is Alphonzo also, he look fighting mad. I know he is ready to kill someone over his favorite cousin Shaymin.

"Yes Roché," Roger responded somberly, "and not only am I

here to see her, I am here to take care of her for the rest of her life. I have every police officer on the force pulling extra hours to find the cruel person who would commit such a horrible act. I promise you and Shaymin when we get him he will spend the rest of his life behind bars, if I don't request capital punishment for him. Now that is a promise to Shaymin's girlfriends and to Shaymin my wife…"

Roché and Ashley looked at each other as if they had seen a ghost…

Chapter Twenty-Six

SHAYMIN was in a coma for seven days and Roger spent at least ten hours of each day in the hospital right at Shaymin's bedside. He acted as if he was her husband. He must have felt obligated to Shaymin, because he made sure her room was secured at all times and that only a limited number of people were allowed to go in and visit her.

"Roger," Shaymin said. She slowly tried to open her eyes and tried pulling the tube out of her throat.

Roger quickly jumped up and said, "Oh no baby, don't move so fast. Let me get the nurse." He called out, "Nurse, nurse, my baby is coming to. She is trying to remove the tubes in her nose and throat. Please come now."

"Why am I here?" Shaymin asked. Her speech was very slurred; however, Roger was able to understand what she was saying.

"Shaymin baby, you have been injured, but don't think about that right now, just get well. We will discuss this later."

Roger tried to comfort her by holding her hand and massaging her temples.

"Roché! Ashley!" Roger called as he stepped into the waiting room. "She is awake," he announced. Roché and Ashley hurried in to see Shaymin.

"Jesus," Shaymin tried to speak. "Ashley, Roché, why am I here?"

"Shaymin," Ashley said, "don't try to talk, just get well; as soon as we get you better we will talk, but right now just focus on getting better."

Two weeks later Shaymin was released from the hospital and was going home. She was been raped, she had suffered a broken arm, a broken leg, some fractured ribs, and a slight concussion. Now she was going home and Roger promised everyone that he would take care of, for the rest of her recuperation period As Roger reflected on what was in his heart, he began to write:

"The Shaymin Rose"

I give to you this precious gift
For I have nothing but this to give
A Rose I hold in simple hands
To signify my love within

So hard it was to choose just one
For many held the beauty of you
But the one reflected your colors made
The Shaymin Rose the gift for you

L. Charmane Pough Chestnut

But oh, how it caught my eye ablaze
With color apart from the rest
Reduced me to a breathless sigh and
Lured me with its lovely scent

So I chose this Shaymin Rose
Its tender petals silken smooth
And with it gives this fragile heart
And with it give my love to you

Love, Roger!

Roger left the poem, a picture of Shaymin, and a rose lying on her nightstand to symbolize that she is truly the Shaymin Rose.

Shaymin lay in bed and reflected on the words Lady Shelton spoke to her: "If God allowed it, that means He has a purpose." Shaymin picked up the poem and began to read; realizing as she did that Roger truly cared for her no matter what his situation was at home. She believed Roger truly loved her. As tears began to stream down her face, she placed the poem near her heart, looked up toward heaven, and said, "Thank you Jesus. I won't complain."

December Thirty-First

Pastor Shelton began to sing, "God has been so good to me; my good times outweigh my bad times and I won't complain." Pastor Shelton then asked, "Is there anyone who knows that God has been good to him? Is there anyone here who would like to start the New Year off with Jesus being the center of her joy? Is there anyone here who knows that Jesus loves him? Please step out. Is there anyone here who needs

Jesus in her life? Step out please."

Shaymin stepped out of her row and began to walk toward the front of the church. After Pastor and First Lady Shelton led Shaymin to Jesus Christ, Shaymin turned around to return to her seat and saw Roché and Roger standing right behind her. Roger held out his arms and embraced Shaymin and they both began to cry and sob uncontrollably.

Ashley ran around the church. She was very elated that Roger, Shaymin, and Roché all accepted Jesus as their personal savior on December 31. When she finally got her composure back, she shouted, "The angels rejoice when one soul is saved, but three of them at one time—oh my, they are throwing down big time in heaven now."

"Hallelujah!" shouted Shaymin.

See 1stWorld Books at:

www.1stWorldPublishing.com

See our classic collection at:

www.1stWorldLibrary.com

www.ingramcontent.com/pod-product-compliance
Lightning Source LLC
Chambersburg PA
CBHW030515260626
47157CB00005B/1751